With fresh tears filling her eyes, Mae looked up at Jacob.

She watched him as he approached, never moving her gaze away from his. Sitting down gently beside her, he wrapped his arm around her because it was the only option that presented to him. Just was no other course of action.

And when she leaned against him, he took her weight, naturally, as though he'd done so regularly.

Instead of never.

Her warmth, her softness, even her chemical scent engulfed him in a sense of rightness.

"I'm right here," he told her. Jacob knew he was absolutely right to be sitting there. Holding Mae.

Absorbing however much he could of whatever had become her last straw.

As her tears quieted, he continued to hold on. He couldn't abandon her.

She looked up at him, and his hand lifted to her face. He wiped the tears from her cheeks, staring into her eyes. Telling her with everything he had that she was valued.

And more, that she wasn't alone.

Dear Reader,

Welcome to Dark Canyon! I know this place well! In one case, too well. Years ago, I went with a friend to drop our daughters off at a summer camp and then hike this canyon. (Known by another name, but a very real place in southern Utah.) We set out all full of ourselves for a rare day just to ourselves with no one expecting us anywhere. The first hours were all we'd imagined they would be. Unbelievable natural beauty and much-needed conversation about everything under the sun.

Until we realized we were lost. It was late afternoon by then. No one knew where we'd gone. No one was expecting us back. I will never forget those seconds that seemed like hours and hours that seemed like days. I relived the sense of hopelessness warring with determination every day as I wrote this equally engulfing book. The desperation and determination on these pages are real.

And...I'm here to write this, my 140th published Harlequin book! To write this letter. Because believing in yourself, in the spirits around you, and in the love that will hold you in the tough times, brings miracles in real life, too. Not just on the pages of romance novels.

Tara Taylor Quinn

COLTON'S CODE RED

TARA TAYLOR QUINN

Special thanks and acknowledgment are given to Tara Taylor Quinn for her contribution to The Coltons of Dark Canyon miniseries.

Recycling programs for this product may not exist in your area.

ISBN-13: 978-1-335-47195-6

Colton's Code Red

Harlequin Enterprises ULC
22 Adelaide St. West, 41st Floor
Toronto, Ontario M5H 4E3, Canada
www.Harlequin.com

HarperCollins Publishers
Macken House, 39/40 Mayor Street Upper,
Dublin 1, D01 C9W8, Ireland
www.HarperCollins.com

Printed in Lithuania

1 2 3 4 5 6 7 8 9 10 LIT 28 27 26 25

A *USA TODAY* bestselling author of over one hundred and thirty novels in twenty languages, **Tara Taylor Quinn** has sold more than seven million copies. Known for her intense emotional fiction, Ms. Quinn's novels have received critical acclaim in the UK and most recently from Harvard. She is the recipient of the Readers' Choice Award and has appeared often on local and national TV, including *CBS Sunday Morning*. For TTQ offers, news and contests, visit tarataylorquinn.com!

Books by Tara Taylor Quinn

Harlequin Romantic Suspense

The Coltons of Dark Canyon

Colton's Code Red

Mitchell Family Secrets

Shadowed Past
Guarded Past

Sierra's Web

Her Sister's Murder
Mistaken Identities
Horse Ranch Hideout
Cold Case Obsession

The Coltons of Owl Creek

Colton Threat Unleashed

The Coltons of Alaska

Colton's Secret Weapon

Visit the Author Profile page
at Harlequin.com for more titles.

For all those who have the courage to try,
the strength to endure and the faith to believe.
May you never run out of happy endings.

Chapter 1

He hated to wake her in the middle of the night. But Jacob Colton didn't even hesitate as, already in his green pants and gray shirt, he held his phone to his ear on his way out the door.

"Yeah." Dr. Mae Copeland's greeting was about the same as always. Didn't matter what time of day it was. She sounded ready to go.

"Noah was doing a night training session in the canyon. Found a backpack. Female owner based on contents. No ID." Jacob's little brother, a K-9 trainer, had praised his dog's superior night vision for having spotted the thing.

"You have it?"

He was already out in the garage attached to his condo, climbing into his dark SUV, as he said, "Noah's meeting me at the office in five."

Mae, their gifted forensic scientist, lived in an apartment close by. "I'll be there," she said and hung up on him.

Leaving Jacob to speed through the deserted streets of Dark Canyon stuck in his own thoughts during the entire four-minute drive. His heart was heavy.

Were they looking at yet another woman, either on the run from kidnappers intending to sell her into human trafficking or having already been captured by them?

No identification certainly pointed to it looking like one or the other way.

Five months he'd been working this case, along with tribal and local law enforcement. *His* case. He had to end it.

His youngest sibling was already in the lot when Jacob pulled in. Noah's expression serious, he met his brother's gaze, and, without a word, handed over the evidence, then turned and went back to his truck. The dog sitting upright and tall on the passenger seat appeared almost human. Noah certainly treated the very special canine as though he was as much a man as any of them.

Jacob didn't wait to watch the vehicle off the lot. He was already inside the door of the National Park Service's Investigative Services Branch building by the time Noah's taillights disappeared. But he turned back in time to see Mae's headlights coming toward him.

Waiting, the makeshift evidence box Noah had handed him between both hands, Jacob used his shoulder to push against the door to open it as one of his favorite fellow employees hurried toward him.

Favorite because Mae was more like him than anyone else around. Married to the job. Committed 24/7. And happiest that way.

With her long brown hair up as usual in some kind of clip, she barely spared him a glance as she led the way to her lab, unlocking it and heading in first, leaving him to follow.

"Good morning to you, too," he said, mostly just to

connect. And to avoid the tension forming a rock in his gut as he waited to see what Mae might turn up with her machines and magic touch.

Sliding her arms into a white lab coat over her jeans and dark brown T-shirt, Mae nodded, pulled on exam gloves, and reached for the box. Jacob set it on the large metal table in front of them, donning his own set of gloves.

No way was he leaving without cataloging every spec or stray string attached to the inside of the light purple pack.

They worked silently. Lining up the pack's contents carefully. And by the time Mae was treating the pack itself for fingerprints, inside and out, before moving on to the contents, Jacob was breathing somewhat easier. Not a lot. But some.

"It doesn't look like one of our fosters," he said. The kidnappers targeted women who'd aged out of the foster system and were on their own as they didn't have families to come looking for them, or report them missing.

Mae barely missed a beat in her administering to her duties as she rolled her eyes at him. "You might want to wait on the facts," she muttered, as she lifted what appeared to be a decent set of prints from the inside of one of the two main straps along the back of the pack.

His job was to take what he knew and assess. Ask the mental questions. Make educated assumptions and pursue them to the best of his ability until the next pieces of information came to light. Either through Mae's lab or any other lead he managed to come up with, or be given, on a case.

"The packets of hiking food, the condom…" He let

the words trail off as he looked over the items laid out before him.

After taking a photo with his phone, he moved to his text app, opened his own contact, and made a list of the items, texting it to himself, before saying, "Let me know the second you find something," and leaving the lab.

Jacob wasn't at all surprised by Mae's lack of response. The woman was a godsend in every way. The best at her job. And, like Jacob, just wanting to get on with it. She didn't need to chat, shoot the breeze, or talk about the weather.

Mae, in spite of her tall slim build and exotic dark-eyed looks, was all business, just like him.

Mae heard the door close behind Jacob with a hint of relief. Mixed with a tad bit of disappointment, too. The man's lack of patience in waiting for her results before jumping to conclusions on a case was a bit irritating at times, but of all the agents she'd worked with over the past few years, he was the one she enjoyed partnering with the most. And, were she being honest with herself, which she always was, she'd admit the man's assumptions were annoyingly correct a lot of the time.

She wasn't so sure he'd be right on that early-hour morning, however. Most particularly as, not long after Jacob left her lab, she got a hit on the most promising fingerprint she'd found. She had others to run. And would find more as she got to the items inside the pack. Along with, she suspected, other evidence. She already had a test running on a brown spot on the corner of the condom box, suspecting that it might be blood.

But she was on the phone, staring at her results as she waited for Jacob to pick up.

"What do you have?" he asked by way of greeting. Getting right to the point. Of which she approved.

"Male," she gave him the bad news. And then the worst. "Eighteen, from Oso, has a record for petty theft."

Which meant a police connection. And a young thug who'd be willing to do a job for a dirty cop for the right kind of money. A new hire as the previous such no-goods had just been killed.

Jacob had a dirty cop in custody, one they'd just arrested, who had ties to the trafficking ring. Jacob had been certain he'd get the man to talk. It hadn't yet happened.

Then, the Oso component. Another victim had lived in the nearby small town.

"Name." Jacob's tight-lipped response was exactly what Mae had expected.

She was ready for him. "Peter Quincy." She rattled off an apartment address.

And wasn't surprised, silently wishing him success and safety, as she heard his phone click off.

Jacob had a couple of local deputies haul Quincy's butt out of bed and deliver him to a small interrogation room at ISB before dawn.

He'd have preferred to let the punk sit and stew, without the coffee he'd requested, except that Jacob might only have a few hours to find the woman whose backpack was in Mae's lab before the victim was shipped off to Mexico. After which point, according to recent history, she'd never be heard from again.

He shut the door with force as he entered the room. Turned on the recording device that connected through the building's wireless internet system to Mae, in the lab. Allowing her to listen in and act upon any information she might hear that would prove helpful to her.

Then, standing, with both hands on the table, right in front of the younger man, Jacob nearly spit the words, "Where is she?" While he would not break the law, wouldn't physically harm the suspect, he didn't hold back any of his vehemence.

With a quick shake of his disheveled bedhead, the young man's gaze darted around Jacob's broad shoulders, obviously avoiding his angry expression, as he asked, "Who?"

Jacob threw a printed photo of the light purple backpack on the table.

Saw the kid blanch as he glanced down. A clear sign of recognition. "You have thirty seconds to tell me who she is."

"I don't have any idea what you're talking about," the suspect said, his voice gravelly as he stared downward.

Maybe he was looking at the photo lying there. Jacob suspected otherwise. The kid couldn't look at him, or that photo.

He was involved. Even if he hadn't kidnapped the woman, he knew something.

Shoving the photo closer, right under the kid's nose, he said, "Your prints are all over that bag." At least one of them had very clearly been there. "How do you think we knew who to bring in?"

Quincy shook his head. "I don't know anything," he repeated. Multiple times. Showing more and more fear, and agitation, with every threat Jacob made over the next ten minutes. Forcing Jacob to conclude that whoever Peter Quincy was working for scared the young adult more than a federal agent could.

Jacob had to change his tactics. Quick.

Telling the kid to stay put—not like Quincy could go anywhere in the small, windowless space, with a locked door between him and anywhere else—Jacob walked out.

Mae heard it all from her lab. And was waiting when Jacob showed up less than a minute after he'd left the interrogation room.

"I need you to talk to him," he said, as he came in the door. "No one else is here this early, and we might not have any time to waste. The others were left in the house when they were first taken, but that's burned down, and we have no way of knowing if there's another. Or how much of a part dirty cop Olsen played, since he's not talking yet, either. Could be there's no stop-off at this point."

He'd reached her area of the lab, but was pacing. Putting a hand on his arm, Mae told herself that the warmth that settled in her at the touch had only to do with the cold air in the lab so early in the morning, and the temperature of Jacob's skin. And then lost the sensation completely as she concentrated on the only thing that mattered right then.

"I found tears all over the pack, Jacob." Holding the empty bag up with her gloved hands, she made a circle around both areas that had been saturated, as well as the cleaner space in between them. "I also found a small strand of hair, here," she added, pointing to the non-tear space. "It's like she used the pack as a pillow. Lying on it while she cried."

He stared at the pack. And then at Mae. His gaze direct and pointed. "She still had the pack when she was crying," he stated what, in one way, was obvious.

"She hadn't yet been stripped of personal belongings. Items by which we can identify her or her abductor," he said slowly. Then added, "He lost her out there. He had her pack. She got it back. And ran."

Mae nodded. "That's the way the evidence currently points."

"He's scared because he only has a small window of time left to produce her, and he has no idea where she is."

Mae shrugged. She couldn't say. There were no facts to prove that assumption.

Jacob was halfway around the table before he stopped, suddenly. Frowned. Looked at Mae and said, "Then why was he home in bed, asleep, rather than out looking for her? Or on the run from whoever hired him?"

"Yep," Mae said, her lips pursed. Just as one of the screens in front of her flashed up a result. Shocked, she stared, then looked over at Jacob.

"Kelcy Ann McClintock? The daughter of that minister from Wilson who started the theater group for high school kids? His wife's a pediatrician…"

"That's what it says. Her DNA is in a bone marrow donor database…"

Jacob was out the door before she could give him the rest. Picking up her phone, she pushed his speed dial and when he answered said, "Her parents reported her missing yesterday morning. She wasn't in her room when her mother went to wake her up. The bedroom window was unlocked, and not quite shut. As though someone had opened it and closed it behind them. Perhaps with the intent to climb back in."

Jacob burst into the room.

"You took the wrong woman, Dirtbag." He slammed his hands down on the table as he bent to put his face close to Peter Quincy's.

The kid jumped. Was visibly shaken. And seemed clearly confused, too. Tweaking, Jacob surmised. Explained the bed thing. He'd passed out mid-job. Or mid-running from a failed job.

If Jacob wasn't so het up, he might have felt a twinge of pity for the punk.

Remembering his earlier calculation—that Mae would be a better interrogator because Jacob had used the wrong approach—he calmed.

Pulled out a chair and sat down. He needed the forensic scientist in her lab. Doing her magic.

"We just got an ID on the girl you took," he said calmly, glancing from the kid to his own hands clasped together on the table in front of him. "She's not the foster you were after, man," he broke the news with a note of sympathy in his voice.

He had to get the guy to tell him where he'd left the McClintock girl. She'd been missing almost twenty-four hours. In the Dark Canyon Wilderness. With ruthless kidnappers still on the loose.

"Wait." Quincy glanced up at Jacob, actually meeting his gaze.

Jacob held on to it. "I'm waiting."

Leaning forward, Quincy said, "Did you just say that

her parents reported her missing?" He sounded incredulous. As well he should. For a screwup, the guy had managed to outdo himself on that one.

Maintaining eye contact, Jacob gave a slow nod, when what he wanted to do was reach over the table, grab the guy beneath his ears, and lift him up until he begged for mercy. Or rather, spilled his guts.

The blood had drained from Quincy's face. But instead of looking like he was about to pee himself, he seemed to have turned his fear outward. More like worry. "They don't know about me?" he asked.

The question wasn't one Jacob had expected. "No, why? Should they?"

"Oh God." Peter buried his forehead in his fist. "She's my girlfriend," he spilled rapidly, staring Jacob in the eyes. "Her parents don't know about us. They wouldn't approve because I have a record. I took some food a few times," he said. "I've been on my own for the past year… working and finishing high school… That's where I met Kelcy, at school. We've been together almost a year. I thought her parents had sent you after me."

Jacob cared, on one level, but not the current one. "Where is she?"

With moisture filling his eyes, but a clear sense of standing up rather than shriveling in fear, Peter said, "I don't know, man. I thought she was at home. Hating me. Telling her parents about me. When I didn't hear from her all day yesterday… I've been expecting the cops to show up and haul me in."

Right. Gear shift. Immediate.

He needed the kid's help. "Where did you last see her?"

Peter looked lost for a split second as he looked at Jacob, then said, “Dark Canyon Wilderness. It was our graduation gift to each other. We were going to do it for the first time.”

Jacob’s eye roll just happened. As though Peter Quincy was a younger brother that he’d given a hard time during a mishap. More than once.

“I know,” Peter said. “It was stupid. But the idea was hers. Not that I argued. At all. It’s just, her dad’s so strict. We’re both adults.” With a quick head shake, he said, “She came up with the idea to sneak out just after midnight. We’d get to the canyon, do the deed, and she’d be back in her bed before morning.”

“So what went wrong?” Jacob’s clock was ticking. He could sympathize later. If compassion was in order.

“She changed her mind. Said she needed some time alone. She had the car keys. She’d tucked them into a little purse thing she keeps in her backpack. She didn’t want to risk them falling out of my pocket and us getting stranded up there. That’s how she is, always looking out for danger and making sure we avoid it. Which was why the elaborate plan to…you know… She figured Dark Canyon was one place we could go where her father wouldn’t have eyes. Or cameras. Or the ability to trace a credit card.”

All good to know. To piece together the situation. Not pertinent in the immediate moment.

“I need to know what happened, Peter.” Dread was slowly filling Jacob’s gut. The girl had been hurt. He hoped to God she hadn’t been…

“She freaked out…not on me…on herself. Started crying. Said she loved me, had no idea why she couldn't do it, and needed some time alone. I walked off."

A randy kid who'd been led on… Still… "You just left her up there? In the wilderness?"

"Hell no." Peter's face twisted with disgust at the mere mention of having done so. "We were up on this ledge area. I walked down the back of it a ways, and just sat. Figuring she'd find me when she was ready to go. After an hour passed, and we were getting close to when we had to leave to get her home before her parents found out we were gone, I went back for her. But she was gone. I searched everywhere, a mile out each direction, but she was gone. I went to the car, expecting it not to be there. It was still parked right where we left it. That's when I knew she'd called her parents to come get her. And why I was certain the police were there to arrest me. They had the keys to the car and had left it there as proof. I hitched a ride home. Tried calling her a bunch of times. And then just waited for you all to knock on my door. Which you did. I thought her dad was having me charged with attempted rape or something."

Frustration shot through Jacob. "It didn't occur to you that she could be hurt?"

"I called. I searched. I never saw her backpack. Where was it?" Peter named a somewhat well-known ridge in the canyon, stating it had to be there.

Shaking his head, Jacob stood, his phone already to his ear. He barked orders. And then, hanging up, said, "Come on, we're going to need all the bodies we can get to help search."

The backpack had been found at the bottom of the canyon, not the top where the two had been. Kelcy had to have fallen. Or, more likely, based on the terrain, slid. If she'd tried to make it back up to Peter, she'd only have slid down farther, possibly causing an avalanche. Jacob didn't think any further on that one.

She could also have made it the rest of the way down. As her backpack had.

"You need to show us right where you left your car," he told the young lover. "If we're lucky, that's where she headed."

And if they were extra lucky, they'd find her. Alive.

Chapter 2

Mae was waiting for Jacob when he got back to the office much later that afternoon. He'd come to tell her the details of the successful end to a day that had started out grim. He always gave her that respect when they worked a case together. Good news or bad.

And while she mostly preferred her solitude in the lab, those visits from Jacob were the exception. He didn't try to humanize the science. Nor did he ever put pressure on her to be more than she was. More outgoing. More social. More. More. More.

He'd never once asked her out for drinks when the work was done. She was mostly glad about that, too. They worked together, and workplace relationships never went well.

Besides, she didn't do crushes. There was no logic to swamps of emotion that had no basis in longevity. Crushes came and went. By very definition, they were unreliable. She'd looked up the malady. Not only were crushes brief, they were usually on someone inappropriate or unattainable. And they led people into situations where feelings got hurt. Or left them sitting alone wasting valuable hours, days, months dreaming about something that was never going to happen. Something that, given time, they wouldn't even want to happen. Simply put, there was no point in having a crush on anyone, let alone a man she had to work with long term.

And Jacob didn't do relationships, so their future together was already in its permanent stage.

All of which explained why he was the one law enforcement official, above all, that she liked to see. And work for.

Along with the fact that she always seemed to do her best work for him.

As she'd done that day. She'd already had news for him when he'd called well after lunchtime. She hadn't even given him her usual "Yeah" when he'd said, "We've got her. Conscious. Alert. Broken leg." And then hung up.

Which was why she spoke first, the second she saw him coming through her door just after four. "Quincy didn't do it," she said. "His story checks out."

She'd spent a good part of the day going over all the evidence, and, after involving a local officer and a deputy, had solid proof. "Kelcy purchased the condoms, right there in Oso. Paid cash. They have her on video camera. Only her prints were on them. She intended to have sex when she snuck out of her room that night to meet Peter."

Jacob's calm nod took a bit of her thunder. They'd had a long day. Him more than her since he'd been out in the field, traversing rugged terrain.

"He was in the canyon for hours, just like he said, too. All over the place. I traced the location on his cell phone. And he called the friend right when he said, then was at home until he was picked up this morning. He also during all of that time made multiple calls to Kelcy's phone, which was off. Enough to suggest that he was frantic. Both in the canyon and from home."

"Her phone was crushed during her landslide," Jacob said, taking a stool at her main work counter.

Well, then. He didn't need her giving him good news with which he was already in possession.

Landslide. Obviously, the cause of the McClintock girl's disappearance.

"She'd been sitting on a ledge, which gave way," he said then, watching her as he talked, but not acutely. More like he was watching a television rerun that he'd seen countless times. And while a small part of her could possibly be offended, mostly she was warmed by the familiarity between them. And the inherent safety therein.

Truth was, with Jacob, Mae felt...normal. Rather than the odd bird she'd been ever since she could remember. Even with her own family.

Most particularly with them.

"Noah and his newest trainee took us to where he found the backpack. Peter led us from there, toward the car. She'd attempted to crawl and drag herself toward it. She'd made it a quarter of mile from where she slid down. Quincy was the one who found her. She said she'd known he wouldn't give up on her."

She shook her head, frowning. "But he had."

"Yeah." Jacob's chin jutted in the way he had. "Guess that's something they'll have to work out."

Shaking her head at him, she said, "Or not."

"Without him, we might not have found her."

"True. Being hauled in by the cops to help isn't the same as not giving up on her, though."

She heard his grunt. Accompanied by an eye roll. Before he said, "If not for your quick work this morning, identifying Quincy, that girl likely would have died out there. I owe you one."

Something he told her often. She never got tired of hearing it. And had never cashed in, either. Surely there was enough wealth there for one favor.

As she stood there calculating, still not sure that her "favor" account could cover the ask, Mae was at the do-or-die moment. If she didn't give voice to the question she'd been vacillating on asking him for as long as she could put it off, she'd have irrevocably lost her chance.

"I'd like to collect," she blurted, awkwardly even for her.

Brows raised, Jacob sat back. "You what?"

Busy cleaning one of the machines she'd used that afternoon, Mae glanced down toward her shoulder and over to him. "You said you owe me one. I'd like to collect."

She wanted to procrastinate having to actually do so as well.

Looking perplexed, but also maybe slightly amused, he asked, "Collect how?"

"By asking a favor," she told him, fully focused on the already spotless lens she was cleaning. "A big one."

"So ask." He seemed so unfazed, Mae's surprise prompted her to glance over at him before she could stop herself. And then she had to stand there looking at him, with the ball in her court.

And she wasn't into sports. "There was the DNA testing on baby Gracie, the cause of death for Annie Ross, evidence on Fern. The fingerprints I pulled from Ava's home, the accident we worked that took her fiancé's life." She stopped when, arms crossed, he sat there watching her with a deadpan expression. She had no idea what he was thinking, and while, generally, that wouldn't matter… She'd just trespassed on different ground for them.

Or was about to.

"That's what I'm collecting on," she said then. Looking straight at him. His eyes, not the broad shoulders in the beige shirt, the expanse of chest up against the buttons, or the early morning scruff on his chin, either.

"The favor, Mae."

Oh. Right. "I've got this…thing… I have to go to. It's sort of…mandatory. And I have to have a plus-one. Which I don't. Have, that is. And I don't want one, but if I don't bring one…well… Let's just say it will be much better for me if I do."

"Okay." The response was immediate. So unlike Jacob, who considered every situation as though it was a case to solve. "When and where?" His second question followed the "okay" quickly enough that she was still busy processing the initial response. Could hardly wrap her mind around the second.

"Tomorrow night," she told him the worst first. Because he was going to figure out he was a last-minute date when she told him the what. He'd know she'd have had a lot of time…nearly a year's worth…to find herself a companion for the ordeal. "And at Everson Ranch, just north of Wilson."

"I know where the ranch is." He frowned. "And what it is," he added.

Yeah, she was cooked. No way he was going to want to be her date at what could only be a totally awkward situation for both of them.

With her lips pursed, she lifted her brows and stared at him. Waiting for him to find his way out.

He wasn't leaving. He just kept sitting on her stool—one of them—as though he owned it. Which, technically, he kind of did. More than she did, at any rate. He was a higher-ranking official of the US government than she was.

"Your real date bail on you?"

Frowning, she stared at him. Then put the situation right out there. "What date? You ever known me to have a date?" So there was a bit of irritation in her tone. The situation wasn't easy for her.

And he wasn't making it any easier. "You know, Jacob, when one is doing a favor for someone, in order to do it decently, the one doing the doing should do so with grace and kindness."

"More kindness than whoever your plus-one was supposed to be," he said, in a tone that made her really suspicious that he was enjoying himself at her expense. "I'm guessing, since the shindig is at Everson, which is a fancy event venue, that there will be nameplates at the tables. So at whose name will I be sitting?"

Oh God. The man was too smart for his own good. And, apparently, hers.

"Jacob Colton."

She looked him right in the eye as she made the admission. Which was why Jacob felt the tad bit of flutter inside his gut when he computed the ramifications of the response. Out of respect for her. Not because he, in any way, was a tad bit pleased to know that he wasn't a last-minute fallback.

Didn't matter that it was Mae doing the asking. He just didn't like to think of himself that way.

But to be sure that he wasn't getting even a little bit soft on the forensic scientist, he said, "You told someone I was your date a while ago and are just now getting around to letting me know about it?"

"I was planning to say you were sick, or something."

Interesting. So why hadn't she done so? The investigator inside him asked the silent question. Putting forth the fact that he had to know the answer. And so the interrogation began. "Who's getting married?"

The way those brown eyes peered at him from her exotic-looking features seemed to speak capitulation to Jacob. It was another second or two before she spilled all. "My cousin Matilda. My mom's sister's daughter. She's twenty-five to my thirty. And used to follow me around like a puppy dog, emulating everything I did."

And Mae was feeling bad about the situation because it made her look like an old maid? Which she would never be, even if she remained unmarried at one hundred. He knew better than to voice that thought. Didn't fit in any conversation between the two of them.

"'My cousin' would have been enough of a response," he said as a quick cover for the rest of his thoughts. Which were also not befitting of them. Like the fact that she was actually struggling with the whole thing for some reason. "Remind me to make sure you're never in an interrogation room. Willie could crack you."

Willie was the stray cat that sometimes hung around the ISB building. Their receptionist had named him.

At that last dig, Mae straightened her shoulders, and had the fire back in her eyes—his intent—as she said,

"I'll have you know I've been interrogated multiple times on the witness stand by both the state's top prosecutor and defense attorney, and won the cases, every time."

Yeah, he'd known that, too.

"Claws in, Dr. Copeland," he said, and then, "I'm assuming this is formal? And what time do you need me to pick you up?" He had a smile in his voice. He couldn't help it.

Couldn't really even explain his current state of mind to himself. He had to pay her back for all the extra work she'd done for him recently, professionally and personally. He had to go. Didn't explain why he was kind of looking forward to doing so.

And that was a case that was a mandatory solve before he got his nice duds on and drove the mile or so from his condo to her apartment the next afternoon.

She'd told him to pick her up at two. They weren't due at the well-known event ranch, for the outdoor wedding and then formal indoor dinner and dance reception, until four.

Mae just liked to give herself enough time to deal with any last-minute issues or problems and still be on time. Most particularly when she was dealing with her family.

But if all went as planned, what was she going to do with the man for an hour before the wedding started?

Sit in the bar and drink, the answer presented almost immediately. She'd definitely need a drink to calm her nerves so she could deal with her family.

Especially with a "date" along.

She never should have asked him. The fact had hit her the second she'd heard herself say she needed a plus-one, the day before. And reached critical danger level on Saturday morning when she met up with Sassy Colton, who'd offered to help her find something to wear to the wedding, and do her hair and makeup for her. The owner of the gallery in town, Sassy was also an artist and since Mae had never given any time or attention to her appearance, other than to make certain that she was neat, clean, and appropriately clothed, she'd jumped at Sassy's offer weeks before she'd actually thought about going through with the whole wedding plus-one situation.

Sassy had stopped by the ISB building to drop off food for the staff, mostly her cousin Jacob, who didn't eat the best, when Mae had just come in from a trip home for lunch, and had been looking at the mail she'd picked up. Which had included the wedding invitation.

She hadn't meant to groan aloud when she'd read the details. The date. Location. And had seen the plus-one card. She'd been secretly hoping for a quiet affair for immediate family in someone's backyard.

Nor had she expected her reaction to be overheard by Jacob Colton's cousin who'd been walking in behind her with a thermal bag filled with sandwiches and fruit hung over her shoulder.

Back all that time ago, Sassy had just admitted to having fallen in love with her best friend, Nick, and had been all sunshine and roses about a wedding at Everson. She'd been so genuinely happy about offering to help that Mae—who had few, if any, close friends—had just blurted out her acceptance without any thought to the actual following through on it at all.

And had procrastinated getting it done until the very last minute. Kind of like her invitation to Jacob.

Which was why she was in Dark Canyon's nicest women's clothing shop the morning of the wedding to choose her dress, after which, they'd proceed on to Mae's nondescript small apartment for Sassy's personal attentions to Mae's appearance.

And why she found herself completely frozen, tongue-tied, right there on the carpeted floor of the clothing shop, when Sassy asked, "Are you taking a date to the wedding?"

Wanting to know how sexy Mae should look? As in, was she dressing to get the attention of a man, or just going to a family function?

The question presented in the form of a horror story, and Mae quickly told her, "No," but couldn't lie, and added, "Just someone I know at work, as a plus-one."

What had she done? The question made her skin cold. The wedding was out of town. For Mae's family and her cousin's friends. No one from Dark Canyon would be there.

Or be aware of how closely Mae and Jacob worked together.

Purely professionally. They'd never given anyone any reason to suspect differently.

It sure as hell couldn't start, either. She'd have to quit the job she loved. And leave the only place where she'd ever felt like she belonged—her lab at ISB. And so she changed the subject. Immediately.

Filing through various dress choices, not really caring about any of them one way or another as long as they fit, Mae kept up a steady stream of conversation about the artist from Sassy's gallery who'd been hiding drugs in the gallery so that the drug runner could get them for distribution. Mae had worked the case. It was something she and Sassy had in common. The pair would be going to trial. So it fit that Mae would let the gallery owner know that she was in good hands with Mae. Giving her specifics on the rock-solid evidence she'd present when called upon.

She could also talk about Sassy's near-death experience when she'd been trapped in her car on the bridge that had collapsed over the river a few months before. Just not with as much authority since it wasn't a situation that called for Mae's talents.

As it turned out, Mae didn't need the bridge collapse. She tried on the dress that was Sassy's first choice off the rack—a black-and-white number, slim cut to the calves, with a slit up to mid-thigh—heard Sassy gasp, and made the choice to be done there.

She couldn't do all black. It was a wedding, not a funeral. But since black was her favorite color, the second she'd seen the option with the white satin bow at the shoulder, and white satin piping, she'd known it was something she could actually see herself pulling off.

Since she had to do so. And after calling her cousin to make certain that the little bit of white wasn't off-putting to her, the bride dressed in white, she knew she'd found the one.

The dress was on sale, which was even better.

And most important of all, Mae had managed to sidestep any more questions regarding the person who'd be partnering her at the Everson Ranch that night.

Chapter 3

You could take the investigator to a non-work function. You couldn't take the automatic tendency to investigate out of the plus-one.

Most particularly when he was out of his element.

Pushing back on his automatic instinct to let Mae know she was going to owe him big for the evening, since he was there paying his debt to her, Jacob had no choice but to put on his over-observant, looking-for-answers hat. It was either that or notice how freaking hot the forensic scientist looked when she let her hair down.

Literally. He'd ever only seen Mae's hair up in sedate clips. Had had no idea that her brown hair was so silky looking, or that it hung in waves all the way down to the small of her back. Which had been left exposed by the dress she had on.

Something he hadn't realized until they'd actually arrived at Everson Ranch and she'd taken off the short cover-up thing she'd called a shrug, a movement that had temporarily lifted the hair away, baring that oval cutout beneath her rib cage down to where the top elastic of her underwear would be. If he could see it. The hair had dropped back in place.

It had all been a shock, really, given that the front of the dress had been high-necked and demure looking.

He'd kept his eyes firmly on the road from the second she'd gotten in his SUV. Driving hadn't been enough of a distraction from the woman sitting mostly silently next to him. But it'd had to do. Better that than the opposite—getting distracted by her and causing a wreck.

As Jacob took his seat at the elegant bar next to Mae—stools directly in front of the bartender that she'd chosen over the more intimate tables set around the room—he took the only option left to him and put on his investigative hat. Mae's parents hadn't yet arrived.

And if she'd known others they'd passed on their way straight to libation, neither they nor Mae had given any indication of it.

"You're sure this is the right place?" he asked her as she seemed to give her gin and tonic the same attention she did the slides in her lab.

"Of course I'm sure." She took a sip from her glass, then stared into it some more.

"You don't seem to know anyone." Maybe not polite of him to point out the fact, but then manners had never been big between the two of them. A fact he was fond of.

"My Aunt Susie and Uncle Stan are standing out in the lobby. They were the couple talking to the little girl when we came in. And the parents of the little girl, the father, is their son, Matilda's older brother."

So…the family throwing the wedding. The reason she was there.

And he had to ask, "Are your parents here, too?" Though they were way early, there were others dressed in finery milling around.

"I haven't seen them yet. They'll find me. And you'll know it."

Okay, then. That about wrapped that one up. Mae wasn't close with her family. And yet… She was there. Uncomfortable. Drinking, which was something he'd never seen her do before. But then, he'd never seen her outside of work and drinking on the job was a definite no-no.

"Why did you come?" he had to ask.

She turned toward him then, giving him one of her "What's wrong with you?" frowns, and said, "They're my family. I couldn't not come."

A lot of families who weren't close didn't get together during special occasions. He had some distant Colton relatives in North Dakota that didn't do all of their family weddings. Nor did he travel to theirs.

"Why not?" he asked, out of honest curiosity.

Shaking her head, her attention aimed at her glass again, Mae said, "First, it would hurt them, which I don't ever want to do. And second, they'd worry about me, which means descend upon me, and that I do not need."

Wow. A family that loved each other, and a member of it who shared the love, but didn't want to be a party to it? Jacob didn't get it.

But the investigator in him wanted to.

Mae wasn't hating the night. Her plan to hang out at the bar until it was time to head outside to be seated for the wedding had been a great one. Sitting at the end of the bar, with Jacob on one side of her and the wall on the other, had precluded anyone from coming up to say hello. They'd have had to talk to her back.

Have her looking over her shoulder.

And they could all talk with her later anyway.

There were a few hiccups when she caught herself, and then Jacob caught her, looking him over. But then she'd blurted the truth of what she was thinking, "I like you better in your uniform with scruff on your chin," to cover up for the fact that his fancy suit and shiny shoes were drawing her attention and the attention every other woman in the room seemed to be giving him. And more to the point, to distract her from the decidedly odd negative emotions rising up in her due to the other women in the room looking him over. She couldn't be jealous where Jacob Colton was concerned.

He didn't seem to be noticing the other women. At her 'out there' comment about his appearance, he just rubbed his chin, grinned at her, and gave her a playful punch on the arm.

While she'd managed to avoid speaking to any of her relatives before the wedding, conversation at dinner couldn't be helped. But as it turned out, she and Jacob had been seated with the two cousins from hers and Matilda's mothers' older half brother, and their spouses. The boys had always been kind to her as a child, and she hadn't seen either of them since she'd graduated high school.

They didn't know her well enough to be aware of her lack of dating, or any serious relationship, ever. Or didn't care.

And Jacob had been the star of the show. As soon as Emory and Benton had heard who he was, they'd been barraging him with questions about the suspected human trafficking ring being run through the Dark Canyon Wilderness, on the way farther south to the Mexican border. And good guy that Jacob was, he'd included a lot of Mae's work in the bit of retelling he could do.

Instead of looking like the freak she was to her family, she'd come across like some kind of rock star. To a distant branch. But still… It was nice. So much so that the feeling lingered once the meal was over and everyone moved into the party portion of the evening.

The real Copeland celebration.

Which, meant, a free-for-all. The duties were over. People could leave their assigned places and move about as they pleased. And her parents, as a united front, made a beeline to meet Jacob.

Barely looking at her—after including her in a warm glance and their in-unison "Hello, you two"—they engaged Jacob in conversation that ended up being similar to what had transpired over dinner. The digest version.

And then her mother looked at her and said, "Are you doing okay, Mae?"

"Fine, Mom." Her answer was always the same.

"And dinner was okay? I was worried about you making conversation with Emory and Benton."

Cringing inside, Mae included both of her parents in a look as she said, "No worries. Jacob handled it all for me."

Smiling, her mother laid a soft hand against Mae's cheek and said, "Well it's good to see you, sweetie. You look wonderful, by the way." Then she leaned in to say, loud enough for Jacob to hear, "You should do your hair and makeup more often. I hardly recognized you when I first came in."

"Yeah, well, Mom, I can't have mirrors in the lab.

The reflection would scare all the little mites that show up on my slides."

As usual, her mother, taking her seriously, shared a glance with her dad, then said, "Yes, dear. Well, you two have fun tonight," and off they went. With backward glances at Jacob.

Hoping he'd marry her and take care of her for the rest of her life so they could be assured she wouldn't grow old alone. Or something. Truth was, she didn't really have any idea what her parents wished. Other than that she'd be more…like them.

Less obsessed with finding the cause of deaths. Or identifying strains of odd things that could prove exactly where a particular leaf or blade of grass came from.

They didn't get that she liked to read horror books, either.

Ultimately, they just wanted her happy. She believed that with all her heart. They just didn't understand how she could be, with the life choices she'd made.

Her two younger brothers, both farmers like their dad, weren't much better when she and Jacob came upon them, with their wives, at a tall table off one side of the dance floor.

"Hey, sis, who's your guy?" William, the older of the two, asked.

And once again, she introduced Jacob. And then just stepped back, letting him take over the conversation without even trying to pretend that she wasn't doing so.

Which left her open to William's wife leaning over to her and saying, "You look fab, Mae. Best ever. Who did your hair and makeup?"

At which Mae smiled back and said, "I bought this robot that you can program, through pictures you choose from a database, to do you up exactly like the photo. You just have to be sure to sit just right or you could end up with eye makeup on your cheeks or forehead." Because, what? Whoever made her look good couldn't have been a science nerd like her.

She felt Jacob's appreciative huff in response to her humor, and was better able to endure the look of discomfort on her sister-in-law's face as she turned back to the conversation going on at the table.

Just another awkward moment with Mae around. Clearly, when her parents' genes had been passed out, Mae had missed the small-talk one.

Funny, Sassy didn't seem to have problems conversing with Mae. But then the artist had inner vision. An ability to see on a deeper level than most. Which would make her better suited to discern Mae's intent. Less dependent on verbal expression.

Or at least be able to tell when Mae's dry sense of humor was on stage.

Still, all in all the evening went far better than she'd even dared to hope. Jacob was damned good company, but she'd already known that part from their hours spent privately debriefing cases in her lab over the past couple of years. Nice to know, though, that her enjoyment of him carried over from her lab to the outside world. And he didn't like to slow dance, which precluded any awkward moments there. He actually made her laugh a time or two when, had she'd been alone, she'd probably have been tense enough to snap.

As hard as she tried, she just couldn't get it right with those she loved the most. And so…she loved from afar.

And overall, she was good with that.

* * *

By the time Mae signaled that she was ready to leave the wedding reception Saturday night, Jacob was eager to get her out of there. He'd seen enough to form some pretty heart-rending conclusions about Mae Copeland.

He wanted the case closed. For her sake.

Which he turned to do as soon as he pulled up to her apartment and put the SUV in Park.

She had her hand on the door, but frowned when he said, "Hang on a second."

They'd talked on the way home. Mostly her, giving him the rundown of everyone he'd met that night. Information that would have been nice to have had in his possession prior to the event, rather than afterward.

He didn't tell her so. The woman had had enough negative reinforcement in those few hours to last most people a year or two. Maybe even a lifetime.

Her family clearly felt threatened by their inability to understand her. Didn't mean anything was wrong with her. But being around them with her, it certainly made one feel as though Mae was somehow lacking.

Enter Jacob.

"I just have to say…back there…their inability to get you… It's not a reflection on you, Mae." As awkward as he felt with deeply emotional topics of conversation, he was prompted from the inside to get it out. "I, more than anyone, know how very much you outshine pretty much everyone else around."

Her eyes narrowed, but she was staring at him like she wasn't quite convinced, or something, and he pushed forward. "So you're not like them. It's okay to be different, Mae. Better than okay, you… You're special for a reason. You've got a gift, a special kind of sight, a mind that's able to understand intricate things most people don't even know are there."

The tight set of her shoulders didn't seem to be softening at all. "They just don't understand, but I'm sure they want to. Bottom line, it was clear that they all love you very much. And are proud of you, too." Truth. Every word of it.

Jacob sure admired the hell out of her. Always had.

Which was why he spent far more time in her lab than his job required.

"I rely on you more than anyone else to help me catch the bad guys," he told her with a bit of a grin. Trying to lighten the moment even while he attempted to make a bone-deep uncomfortable situation better for her.

And then, his expression dead serious, he ended with, "You save lives, Mae. And prevent deaths, too. There's nothing else you could be doing that would ever live up to that."

She nodded. Met his gaze briefly. Then opened her door and got out.

"Thanks for coming with me tonight," she told him. "Your debt is paid in full."

She shut the door. He watched her walk up to her place. Head inside. Waiting for a wave. For something.

She didn't look back.

A pat on the back. He'd given her a damned pat on the back.

There was a reason she'd never seen him outside work. Why her life and her family were kept completely separate. Always.

She fit well into the world she'd made for herself. Outside it, not so much. And she'd just as soon no one in her daily life knew that.

It was her fault, really. She'd known she shouldn't have asked Jacob to attend the wedding with her. Which was why she'd put off the asking for so long.

And then…after a long day of work, with a happy ending for once, she'd had a thought of the wedding looming the next day, accompanied by a return of the dread that always involved time with family, made that much more acute by the fact that she'd blurted out Jacob's name as a plus-one during one of her last visits home, just to get out of the bad moment she'd been in with her mother. A choice she'd regretted the second she'd heard the words come out of her mouth.

Just like she was currently railing against the regrettable decision that had grown from that weak moment with her mother. The invitation she'd issued in another vulnerable second.

Which was why she knew not to ever let herself feel vulnerable when around others.

Okay. Mistakes had been made. Price had to be paid.

But that…pep talk he'd given her…like she was what, ten? A kid needing a hug?

Now, if Jacob had looked at her and had seen a sexy woman he'd wanted to hug…no. Force stop. The thought was an anomaly. A skewed impression born from the myriad emotions that always hit when she was with her family, combined with all the visual attention she'd seen Jacob garner the night before.

There'd been a lot of beautiful, unattached women there. At least two of the bridesmaids, front and center.

One of which had been looking at Jacob all through the wedding.

As though the woman sitting next to him—Mae—hadn't counted as viable competition. Because her cousin had filled the woman in on her weird older cousin who had no interest in men?

Not true. But somewhat Mae's fault that the thought floated among her family members. She'd sort of put it there. Allowed it to flourish.

As a way to get them all off her back about her non-existent love life.

To his credit, Jacob hadn't seemed to notice any of the women vying for his attention that night before.

None of which mattered at all to her current predicament. She needed a way to move forward.

And there was only one penance that would eradicate any chance of a repeat of Jacob's attempt to shore up a woman who was only allowed to bolster herself.

She had to give up all superfluous conversation with him. No more moments with him sitting on a stool next to hers in the lab, or coming down to debrief.

The first was easy enough to accomplish. First thing Monday morning, Mae removed the extra stool from her space. Stashing it in the very back of a storage room off the lab. And then piling boxes on top of it.

She'd ruined their easy camaraderie. Leaving herself no option but to step away from it.

Period.

Chapter 4

First thing Monday morning, Jacob went down to Mae's lab, to check in with her. He had critical business. But he also was carrying around an odd pressure egging him to make sure she was none the worse for wear from the wedding.

And to keep things on their regular footing. Except that…she wasn't there.

Which was already unusual. And had his investigator radar beeping.

It took only a matter of seconds to see the storage door open in the back of her lab. He headed there, thinking he'd offer assistance if she needed some heavy lifting done. But stopped cold when he heard what was clearly a sniffle.

And then another. There'd been no sneeze. And the sounds were accompanied not by a nose blow, or quiet, but by breathing that very clearly stipulated soft sobs.

A variation of crying, at any rate.

Hurrying forward, following his first instinct to rush in and find out what was wrong, to save the day as he'd done so many times with his younger siblings and cousins—and with his father after his mother had died—Jacob came to a dead stop a few feet from the door.

If she was physically hurt, Mae would be calling for help, not quietly crying in the darkest corner of her lab.

And if she wanted company, she wouldn't be hiding in the darkest corner of her lab.

She had his cell number. Had never been shy about using it. In anger, joy, frustration, victory, fear… She'd sent them all his way.

But never tears.

Those were hers to share or not. And clearly she was choosing not.

Deeming them off-limits.

So Jacob did the only thing he could think of in the moment. Driven by an uncomfortable energy he didn't understand, a need to reach out to Mae in what was most certainly a critical—if private—moment, he pulled out his phone and was already sending a text before he was even outside the lab.

Decomposed, unidentified female body found in national park near Mexico border. Arrived early this morning. Tattooed. Evidence of having been chained.

And hit Send.

No matter what was upsetting Mae, she'd respond.

Business always came first. With both of them.

On it.

Mae sent the text to Jacob within seconds of her phone vibrating against her thigh from inside the pocket of her lab coat.

The ME got the body first. Mae didn't wait for evidence to arrive in her lab. Ten minutes after she'd had the text from Jacob—having wiped her eyes and dabbed her face with cold compresses—she was in Autopsy with her handheld XRF spectrometer, analyzing the ink from the woman's tattoo. One that had been similarly placed to Fern's—the victim who'd been rescued just in time by Jacob's cousin Ryan.

Because of decomposition, Mae couldn't tell the shape or colors of the body ink. And didn't need them.

Alone in Autopsy for the moment, she worked efficiently, at her best. Taking explicit photos of the chain indentations noticeable in what was left of the flesh. And doing what she could to attempt fingerprints. She wasn't at all hopeful on that one.

But had several sources of DNA, collected and in small plastic containers, in her evidence box as she headed back to her lab shortly thereafter.

Where once she'd have texted Jacob as every result came through, that Monday she waited until she'd analyzed everything she had before contacting him.

And, with the full report in hand, rather than a quick text telling him to come down, as she'd have done the week before, she simply sent the results.

One text.

A list.

Thanking whatever spirits watched over her, good or bad, that the man hadn't witnessed the shocking, frightening breakdown she'd had that morning. A first, to be sure.

If it happened again, she'd have to call a doctor. Have a full chemical workup to find out what in the hell was wrong with her system.

The catalyst for the tears had been a thought about heading into her workday under a new, non-Jacob regime. But that couldn't have been the cause. Only the match that set off something ready to explode.

Could be hormones. She was thirty. Not giving birth. But not on birth control, either. Unless something was seriously wrong with her, she shouldn't be having hormonal deficiencies or surplus, either.

Not enough serotonin, she could accept, due to the amount of time she spent locked in a windowless lab. But given that she'd been doing so for years, a sudden deficiency wasn't logical.

Telling herself to shut up, Mae checked her results a fourth time. Knew she was right. And, after boxing the evidence, was just back at her computer, ready to run some analyses, when she heard the lab door open.

"Mae?"

Stiffening, she stood, right hand on her mouse, left on the keyboard. Saying nothing. Jacob never called in her name.

But he'd never met her family before, either. Apparently the pat on the back hadn't been sufficient. He was going to be treating her with kid gloves, too.

Obviously, like her, he'd realized that the time they'd spent at that wedding had irrevocably changed who they were to each other.

They'd managed to kill off a several-year close working relationship in the space of hours. Grand.

"You okay?" He came around the corner. She knew because she heard him. She didn't turn around.

The question rattled her some more. He never asked.

He always just peered at her when he came in, drew whatever conclusions he did, and moved on.

He'd gotten pretty damned good at judging her moods, which she'd greatly appreciated.

Her sucky luck that that had been screwed up, too.

"I've done a fourth check," she said, proud of how normal—and unattached—her voice sounded. "Just waiting on DNA to hopefully confirm an identification."

While they couldn't yet prove who was behind what Jacob feared was some kind of human trafficking ring based in the Dark Canyon area, crimes that were involving foster women who'd aged out of the system, Jacob's middle brother, Mark, had pulled some strings to hack into personal records that had garnered them a pretty damned strong-looking suspect. A local man, former Lieutenant Governor Ken Baylor.

The search had netted a list of foster care records and addresses. Some of which matched the women they'd found—one dead, and the other Fern. If they could positively identify another, Jacob and the teams working with him would have a stronger case.

"The tattoo ink matched," Jacob stated a line item in her text. "And the same composition is used commonly by many artists."

She nodded, still scrolling. Not really taking in anything passing before her eyes.

"And the approximate location on the body," he added, standing where his stool had always been.

He didn't mention its absence. She pretended not to notice anything different. In her lab, or between them.

"I didn't expect fingerprints," he said then.

She nodded. It had been a long shot. One that didn't pan out.

Right then, her brain seemed to turn on, and, instead of scrolling uselessly, Mae aligned the mouse, clicked, then repeated the action, bringing up photos on the big screen above her main long metal worktable.

Jacob looked up. Studied the chain impressions visible to him. "The left is from Fern's body," she said, though the photos themselves made it obvious that the left image represented a live body and the right one was very clearly taken of a corpse.

She spoke to fill awkward spaces that were the result of her mistakes. Given time, Jacob would rely more and more on text as their main means of communication. And quit coming down to the lab at all.

Just had to give it the time.

Using her mouse, Mae moved the right image on top of the left. Showing Jacob what she'd found. And had already texted him.

Still, she understood his wanting to see for himself.

"They're exactly the same," he said softly, from closer beside her than he'd been.

She couldn't help turning to look at him. They'd been working the case for five months. Day and night. Mostly seven days a week. Living every moment with the untold number of women who'd been and were still being trafficked.

Women who didn't have families at all.

Made Mae's awkward moments with herself seem as childish as Jacob's pat on the back and kid gloves.

His gaze seemed to grab hold of hers the second she offered hers up. Standing there, she could look away.

But didn't.

Not because she was clinging to what she couldn't have.

But because they were closing in on some morally and emotionally corrupt individuals.

Their shared feelings were intense. But they weren't personal.

It was just a work thing.

His stool was missing. And so was Mae.

Her body was there. Her mind was working. The person he'd grown to value more than any other outside his own family was definitely absent.

Didn't take an investigator to figure out that something was horribly wrong.

And Jacob wouldn't be able to live with himself if he let it go.

Had she been attacked during the night? Her apartment broken into? God forbid, had she been assaulted? Sexually?

There was no physical sign of bruising. But then Mae would know that to fight someone bigger, stronger, and armed would only make her less able to defend herself. She'd use her mind, not her body, to outwit her attacker.

Then, too, Fern hadn't had a single mark on her face. And with the sleeves of Mae's lab coat, he couldn't see her wrists.

He had to see her wrists.

Dammit. He was a top-notch investigator. He had to get her to talk to him.

In all the years he'd known her, all the horrific things they'd seen, the degradation they'd put together, piece by piece, there in her lab, and the woman had never shed a tear.

She'd been doing more than that a few hours before. She hadn't just been letting tears fall. The damned things had been ravaging her.

She'd also done her job that morning. In perfect form. Because the forensic scientist not only believed in what she did, she'd dedicated her life to it. And as such, if she'd been attacked, collecting all evidence would be of utmost importance to her.

The scientist in her wouldn't let her destroy it.

She could have already been to the hospital. Was there a report waiting for him on his desk?

During the many seconds that Mae allowed Jacob to stand there, staring into her eyes, thoughts flew like wildfire, burning through him with a rate of speed that prevented him from stopping them.

Until he was pulled out of the bizarre moment by a series of beeps. He and Mae turned their heads in unison, giving one of her screens immediate attention.

The picture flashing on her screen showed a young blond woman, sweet face, no makeup, or obvious piercings. Long hair. Looked like someone you'd call to babysit your kid, if you had one.

"Maura Bennet," Mae read aloud, her tone low, lacking in any hint of accomplishment or joy in having found the match. "Arrested for protesting outside a women's clinic two years ago." She typed some more. "No missing person report."

Then navigating to another screen, she typed. Pulled up the list he'd have gone to had he been at his desk.

Names from the foster care records found in Ken Baylor's private records.

They were alphabetically arranged.

Maura Bennet was third on the list.

Mae spent the rest of Monday going over every piece of evidence she'd collected from Maura Bennet, as well as other things that had come in from the team at the border and from their own medical examiner.

She couldn't help save the woman's life. But she could, hopefully, trace her tragedy back to its source, and help stop the fiends who were preying on innocent women alone in the world.

Ostensibly they did it for money, and, somewhat, Mae allowed that they probably did. But it took a sick mind, a severely broken person to be capable of the atrocities that were being enacted on these women without parents or other family.

Throughout that day, and the next, Mae stayed focused on finding the answers she was seeking, running every test she knew, and experimented on other possible ways to prove that Maura's body had been near Dark Canyon. Attempting to pinpoint a specific part of the area. Which meant asking for soils and fauna from all different parts of the county. And from the wilderness, too.

If she could give Jacob even a basic geographical radius, he'd be able to narrow down his search. Looking at any traffic cameras in the area. Searching every credit card used at every establishment nearby. Places someone might have stopped traveling to and from. She had to find wherever they met up. Lived. Hid weapons. Stashed money. Or other kidnapping evidence.

The hack that had been initiated into Ken Baylor's personal files had produced a mother lode. And none of it would stand up in court. Or even allow Jacob to obtain an arrest warrant to bring the guy in for questioning. Because the search had been done without a warrant.

Nor had Jacob been able to find any evidence of Baylor having any kind of wealth that would point to the man's illegal activity. No offshore accounts in his name. No big transfers of funds anywhere, other than some kickbacks from prominent businessmen. Which showed him for the slime he was, but the money wasn't enough to make the man rich.

It was up to her to take the legally obtained evidence and use it to home in on something Jacob *could* use. Something that would legally and separately lead them to Ken Baylor.

Like narrowing down the type of chain that had been used on Fern. And going over all the evidence they had on Annie. While she'd been a foster, and had been kidnapped, she'd been left to die of hypothermia in the canyon, not trafficked. Because she'd seen who'd taken her roommate, another foster, Camille. Who had never been found.

Maura had likely been with the kidnappers for longer than Fern. Assuming her body was at all related to a trafficking ring. She was their best lead. The answers were there, she just had to find them.

And she would.

More efficiently and rapidly if she was at her best. Tuesday evening, after a full day of analyzing, surmising, testing, and researching, she was exhausted. More so than normal after a long day. Because she wasn't herself.

Not only was she wasting energy on avoiding any private time with Jacob in the lab—inventing excuses for why he had to leave her alone right then every time he came to see her—she was having to expend far too much determination on avoiding her most personal emotions.

Questions that had been plaguing her most of her life. That had come to the fore with a wham since she'd taken Jacob to Matilda's wedding. He'd seen her. The private woman she'd been her whole life, who was a complete oddity to her family.

And had felt the need to pat her on the back.

Then, the very next time he saw her, Monday morning, he'd asked if she was okay. Because what he'd seen was causing him to view her differently.

Shaking her head as she stood there in her lab well after her shift was supposed to be over, after she'd put away, and properly secured, everything she was working on for ISB, Mae was fighting with herself to the point of being unable to act.

She couldn't leave. Couldn't turn her back and walk away from the search for a very personal answer.

She'd had the evidence for years. Had hated herself for even collecting it. For needing to do so to the extent that she'd taken others' DNA evidence without the owner's knowledge or permission.

When she'd first landed the job at ISB, having her own private lab, she'd gone home to celebrate her dream come true with her parents. They'd been proud of her, of course, but then, they always had been. To the point of taking her science accomplishments for granted.

Her career wasn't what mattered to them, or worried them, about her. As long as she was happy in her chosen field, and it was an honest profession that could pay her bills, they didn't care what she did. What they did care about, and what greatly concerned them, was her perennially single state.

Because they were happily married and considered raising their family the absolute most fulfilling and meaningful part of their lives, because they loved each other and their kids more than anything else, and because they were happiest when they were together with their kids, they'd determined that she needed the same.

And that she just didn't get it because she hadn't yet experienced it.

They didn't get that she simply wasn't like them. She had her highest moments when she found an answer that would save a life. Or prevent more deaths. Nothing else on earth compared to that.

And… She was more comfortable alone. Even her own parents and brothers didn't get her. How could she expect others to do so?

She wasn't good at small talk. She was too intense and ended up finding some deep meaning that, when spoken, caused others to frown at her. Stop talking. Or, most often, change the subject.

And her sense of humor…other than Jacob Colton… no one had gotten that either. She didn't find slapstick funny. Videos of people falling that swarmed the internet as humor, or went viral for their ludicrous content, made her cringe. All she could think about was how the person had to have felt when they were falling. The velocity of the fall, the force of the land, the fear clutching them as they were airborne… That didn't make her laugh.

Her own, slightly macabre way of looking at the

world, of finding humor in outrageous twists on the mundane, fell flat every time. Unless Jacob was present.

All of which he'd witnessed firsthand, and for the first time, at the wedding. The her falling flat part. Her family didn't get her. Didn't understand or share her sense of humor.

He'd seen her as the peculiarity she'd been growing up.

She shouldn't have taken him as her plus one. No argument there. She'd made a colossal mistake. One that was affecting her far more than she'd known on Sunday when she'd summed up the situation, and the price she'd have to pay to move forward.

She wasn't moving forward. She was regressing. Way back to high school. Validating Jacob's treating her like a kid. She couldn't have that.

And the only way forward, logically, was to better understand herself. Scientifically.

The night of her ISB job celebration with her family, she'd surreptitiously collected DNA evidence from all four of them. Thinking there had to be something biologically wrong with her. And then, ashamed of herself for having done so, she'd promptly stored it all in a sealed evidence box in her storage room.

A little box that had prompted the sobs that had burst through, and out of her, as she'd held it, thinking of Jacob's attempt to comfort her the other night. Monday morning's crying jag.

She honestly hadn't even known she was capable of such gross behavior.

And couldn't risk a repeat. If she was going to have uncontrollable body bursts, she'd prefer the flu. Runny nose came with that, too, but there were remedies for it.

Vomiting, the rest of it…all scientifically explainable with commiserate treatments.

When she'd been able to completely separate the life she'd made for herself from the person she'd grown up as, she'd been fine. Happy, even. The parts of her that others found odd just stayed between her and her in Dark Canyon.

Or they had, until Jacob had discovered them at the wedding.

Why she'd ever thought, for one second, it had been a viable solution to take him with her was just another one of the unanswerable questions before her.

Every one of them rested within her. She wasn't finding them.

And the only science she had to seek out was in front of her.

Which of their parents' genetic traits did her brothers have that she lacked? If she knew what set her apart, she could go about finding solutions. All kinds of people in the world had all kinds of issues that they dealt with. From dyslexia to Down syndrome. Addiction to heart disease.

Every bit of it had some kind of basis in genetic makeup. She firmly believed that.

What kind of scientist would she be if she didn't avail herself of every possible chance to find her own answers? What kind of life mate could she be to the person she was if she didn't do all she could to have her own back?

In that moment, the scientist within took over.

And Mae, putting her lab coat back on, got to work.

Strictly for herself.

Chapter 5

It had been a hellish two days. The newly discovered body was producing a mountain of horrendous information, but nothing yet that was getting him any closer to stopping the villains who he firmly believed were stealing the lives of innocent young women, and sending them into purgatory.

Finding out more about Maura Bennet—who she'd been, where she'd lived, whom she'd known, how long she'd been out of the foster system, the office that had been in charge of her younger life, her daily activities, when she'd gone missing, where she'd last been seen and by whom—was vital to the case. And was grueling work.

Jacob, at least, had moments of relief from the relentless investigation. He parried with his brothers. Had lunch with his dad. Was brought a plate of treats by his Aunt Sherry, who was trying so hard to fill the shoes of family matriarch in the four years since Jacob's mother had died.

And the day before had had lunch dropped off to him by his cousin Sassy. She asked where he'd been Saturday night when a bunch of them met in town to hang out. He didn't mention the wedding he'd attended with Mae. No way he was going to open him or his gifted forensic scientist up to the incorrect scuttlebutt such a thing would bring about among his family members, and eventually around town.

It wasn't like he was blind to the fact that women looked at him. A lot. Or deaf to the conversations regarding his bachelorhood. He knew that he was the most sought-after bachelor in the area. He just didn't care.

He had no intention of being anyone's significant other. He wasn't going to sign on to any endeavor in which he'd fail, and that would certainly be one. He was far too protective to be good at letting go, which worked great for his professional life. He dug into a case and held on until he'd taken down the threat. But when dealing with a close one-on-one long-term relationship, he'd likely suffocate with good intention any woman who had the misfortune of him falling for her. He'd be constantly trying to keep her safe without curtailing her freedom to be who she was.

And his work would suffer for it, too.

One man, two masters just didn't work.

But an agent who was concerned for his forensic scientist was a valid part of the one master Jacob did serve. His job.

Which was why, when he saw Mae's vehicle in the parking lot an hour after the sun went down, he headed right back inside the building.

She'd been brushing him off for two days. Granted, the work had been intense, and in overload amounts, but it wasn't the first time they'd been up against such situations. Generally, it was when things got the most feverish that the two of them played off each other best.

Their talking was like a battery charger. He plugged in and had his energy revived.

He'd thought it was the same for her. More than that, he'd been certain that was the case. Just a gut hunch. One he trusted with his life.

So he took his life in his hands and walked purposefully down the deserted hall to Mae's lab, letting himself in with his code on the keypad, without any hesitation whatsoever. If she was in trouble, they all were.

Him, his agents, the local police, and Navajo Tribal Affairs, too. They all came to her table for answers…

His thoughts stopped cold when he saw Mae standing at her table facing dark, totally blank screens. And dread struck his gut when she turned around.

Her face as blank as the screens in front of her, she just…stared. Didn't seem to recognize him, or where she was.

"Mae?" He said her name softly. Taking one step forward, gauging to see if his approach would help or hurt. She was like a frightened animal. He had to help.

Didn't know how to communicate the intention.

And felt acid rising in his chest, too, as he, again, faced the possibility that she'd been attacked sometime between when he'd dropped her off on Saturday night and he'd seen her in her lab Monday morning.

The idea wasn't inconceivable. Someone like Ken Baylor would know of Mae's one-of-a-kind skills. And if he knew they were getting closer to him, would have great cause to stop her from doing the job that was going to prove him guilty of heinous crimes.

Had the man, or one of his flunkies, threatened her? Or her family? While Mae had been awkward around her parents and brothers Saturday night, it had also been shiningly clear to Jacob that she loved them all very much. The way she'd tried so hard—too hard—to be someone they wanted her to be rather than just allow herself to relax and be who she was, was proof of that. The way he'd caught her parents watching her from a distance all night, seeking her out in the crowd, just to see that she was there and okay…

She wasn't.

The silence was going on and on with neither of them moving.

Her a ghost. Him a federal agent with no idea what to do. How to approach her in a way that wouldn't get him a quick stab by the bristles that came out anytime Mae felt as though she wasn't doing her job well enough. Quickly enough. She was her own worst critic.

"Mae?" he softly called again.

She blinked. Didn't even move enough for the hair clasped haphazardly on top of her head to glint differently in the light. Other than the brief eye flutter, she was a human statue. One whose breathing wasn't even apparent.

And that sent Jacob into action. He reached her before the thought to do so had even become fluid.

Taking hold of her wrist in much the same way, he felt for her pulse. Found it alive and well. Firm, strong, and only slightly fast.

As though she was alarmed, but not overly so.

Because she was in shock? How did a pulse react to shock? Where was Nick Malone when he needed him? With Jacob's cousin Sassy, who'd just fallen in love with the paramedic. Sassy, who was also friendly with Mae.

Still holding Mae's wrist—mostly because she hadn't pulled away from him—Jacob reached with his other hand into his pocket for his phone.

Mae's gaze seemed to follow his movement. "No," she said, pulling free of Jacob, stepping back, as though the sight of the phone had brought her out of her stupor.

Because she feared what would happen if he called the wrong person? Or got involved at all?

Jacob knew then what he had to do. There was no other choice.

"Tell me what's going on, Mae, or I make the call." It wasn't like a paramedic and a friendly art gallery owner were going to bring her any harm.

Not that she could know for certain who he'd been about to phone.

Her gaze returned to his. She was there. He could see life in her eyes. And relaxed a notch. But only one.

The life that he saw was shrouded in a darkness he didn't recognize. Or understand.

"Did someone hurt or threaten you?" He couldn't wait around any longer. Had to get to whatever it was she didn't want him to know.

Her head shake was barely that. More a slight movement that could have been side to side if there'd been more of it.

"It's me, Mae." He spread a hand between the two of them. "It's just us here. No recording devices, no one else even in this part of the building. And your lab is soundproof." All information she'd already have. More of a reminder.

She nodded then. A clear motion. Taking the positive reaction as huge, he stepped closer to her again, but kept his hands to himself. Put both of them in the pockets of his green uniform pants. Comforted by the familiar touch of the butt of his gun against his right forearm. There for him the second he needed it.

He was debating whether or not it would serve the interview best if he called her on her crying the morning before, needing to cut to the chase and find out why she'd been so upset, not at all her normal self, treating him differently the past two days, when she said, "No one has tried to threaten me."

He'd asked two things. Hurt and threatened. She'd specified one. Did that mean she'd suffered the other?

Rage coursed through him at the thought. He'd find the thug…and… "What, then?" he asked. Needing to know who to find. And how bad it was going to be for the guy when Jacob got to him. "You haven't been yourself since…" He couldn't mention the tears. No logical explanation within him that went with the knowledge. He just knew. "…yesterday morning," he finished.

She looked up at him, a semblance of the woman he'd come to accept as the most valuable part of his workday, and Jacob took his first easy breath. Mae was still in there. He just had to pay attention. Pick up on all the little clues that led him to successful conclusions.

"I saw myself in your eyes." Her words, when they finally came, were like boulders dropping on the cement floor of the lab. Except that he felt their landing acutely. As though they'd hit him on their way down.

"And that upset you? Knowing how highly I value you?" He didn't get it. But then, other than his mother, when he was young, he'd never been around another woman as many hours in a day as he was with Mae. Wasn't sure of all the nuances.

Which was partly why Mae was so good for him. She didn't need him to get them. "They" didn't need it. They were professionals and so worked just fine in their limited capacity.

The current moment excepted. The moment clearly wasn't professional, and wasn't working out well, either.

"You saw how they treat me. How I am around them. And everyone else, actually, not that you'd know that. And because it was you, someone I bounce ideas off from every day, I saw it, too."

Okay. He was getting a little closer. To at least understanding a topic. Where it was leading, or how it had caused her to sob in her closet, he had no idea. Not even a hint of bridge to get there.

Her next words didn't help much. "I did something I'm not proud of."

The crying. That would definitely not please a woman who prided herself on not seeming at all vulnerable. Jacob knew she was, of course. Just as she knew some of his hot buttons. Came with the territory when you had to deal with heartbreaking situations and gruesome facts day in and day out.

"I'm listening," he told her, walking back his first thought to just admit to her that he already knew she'd had a bit of a breakdown in her storage room. Best to let her give him the parts she felt he had to know. And leave the rest.

"Years ago, during a time when I felt particularly at odds with my family, I secretly collected samples of their DNA, thinking I'd do a full genetic workup, cell by cell if necessary, to find out what made me so different. Where did the dichotomy come to play? I'd be able to weed out all the familial similarities, and work with what was left."

Following her, impressed actually, he raised his brows. Nodding. Eager to hear what she'd found back then. And how it was coming to play in the current situation.

"I didn't have permission to look at them that way, and so I filed the evidence away. Until today."

Today. Tuesday. More than twenty-four hours after she'd been losing it in a dark corner.

Light dawned then. Her seeing herself as she'd supposed he'd viewed her the other night. A past instance where feeling different around her family had brought about a similar internal crisis.

"Because something about this weekend made you need to get those answers," he blurted, greatly relieved to finally be on the right track.

To know that she hadn't been attacked. Though the idea that Ken Baylor could very believably target her was not to be dismissed. Most particularly as they drew closer to nailing the guy.

The twisted jerk went after women. And without Mae's work, Jacob and the others would have to wait months or longer to get even some of the results she turned out so consistently.

Caught up in a very real need to protect his forensic scientist, it took Jacob a second to realize that Mae had glazed over again.

"Hey," he said, drawing closer still. His body wasn't touching hers. That wasn't within their confines. But if either of them breathed too deeply, they'd be breaking that rule. "What's going on here?" His tone had softened.

Maybe more than it should have. Nothing he could do about it after the fact. Nor did he particularly care as concern flared anew within him as her stricken look sent him in another direction entirely.

"You ran the tests," he said.

She nodded. Then said, "Not all of them. Some take days, even weeks…" She was talking. Sounding a tiny bit like herself.

And he had to take the opening. "Are you sick?" he asked. Some slow-moving terminal thing that…

Before Jacob could get any deeper into the theory, Mae shook her head.

"Then what?" he asked, forcing himself not to take a hold of her shoulders. To let her know that she didn't always have to stand alone.

"I'm adopted."

Chapter 6

Mae couldn't wrap her mind around the concept. Good or bad. Right or wrong. Her entire world felt off-kilter.

What was real? What wasn't?

Saying the words aloud to Jacob, the one person who got her, made the situation worse, not better. Had her whole life been a lie?

She'd spent the majority of thirty years blaming herself for being the misfit, when, in fact, she'd just been misplaced. Not in any physical sense. But mentally… If she'd known that one missing piece about herself, she'd have been more understanding. Of her family, certainly. But most importantly, of herself.

She'd always given credence to her parents and brothers, giving them slack when she couldn't just accept their judgment of her. They all blended so nicely together. She'd been the problem. The one mucking up the whole. Not fitting into the family mold.

She had no idea what Jacob was thinking. He hadn't said a word since she'd made her pronouncement. And she wasn't looking at him so couldn't read his expression and body language, either.

He had to go. Her situation wasn't work related. But…

"I'm sorry I used ISB facilities and equipment for personal business," she told him. Acknowledging the inappropriateness of having done so.

Because she didn't want him to go.

When a minute became two, she finally looked up at Jacob. To see why he was still there. And interrupted the strangest look in his eyes—pointed right at her. A mixture of warmth and something else she'd never seen coming in her direction before. Not from him, at any rate.

She didn't know what it was. Felt that it was born of good intention. Kept her gaze locked on his, trying to decipher what he was sending to her. She had to know. They had to work together.

Was he thinking the same things she was? That her oddness maybe wasn't so odd. She just grew up a fish out of water. Since he was the only person in the life she'd built for herself who knew the "other" her, she needed his opinion.

Her earlier mental declaration that they could no longer be close work associates aside. Maybe even obliterated.

"Have you talked to your parents?" His tone, like the looks, was different. She wanted to turn away. To deny him access. And refuse to accept what he seemed to be trying to offer.

For the good of their future working relationship, she had to do so.

And said, "Yes. I ran a rapid DNA test first, before getting into the more complicated and time-consuming breakdowns. Just to set my baselines. When I saw the results, I called them." She'd meant to stop there, but continued right on. "Turns out they'd tried for years to get pregnant. Couldn't. Decided to adopt. And then got pregnant twice, with my brothers." All of which made logical sense.

"And they didn't tell you."

She wasn't surprised that Jacob's summation homed in on the part that she was struggling to accept. "They said that they'd loved me as their own the second I was born. I was handed right to them within minutes of my birth. My birth mother was young. Unmarried. Wanted to go to college. Couldn't care for a child and gave me up. Wanting a clean break. A chance to start again. She never even saw me. I was theirs. We were a family. Then when they got pregnant with the boys they worried that I'd be set apart from the rest of them, and they didn't want that. For me, or for their family. So they kept their secret."

Her parents' motives made sense. If one wasn't Mae, who'd grown up failing to fit her square body into a round hole. Over and over.

Her heart was breaking, but at least she hadn't shed a single tear.

Struggling to wrap her mind around the whole thing, she tried to read Jacob's reaction. Came up with more of the unfamiliar. Because she was outside her whole life looking in? Or because in the space of two days he'd become a stranger?

The second thought was rejected even as it presented. Whatever else happened in her life, even if she had to cut Jacob out of it, he'd never be a stranger to her.

"Aside from the shock, and the hurt, you feeling some relief?" The question stunned her. And hit home, too.

She was in shock. Should have gone straight to that realization the second she'd seen the results.

And… He was right on the other counts, too. Nodding, she held his gaze, looking for more of she knew not what. "I kind of am." She admitted to the relief she hadn't wanted to acknowledge. Then asked, "Is that wrong?"

Chin jutting, he shook his head, seeming more like the Jacob she knew and looked forward to seeing every day.

"I mean, I thought our struggles to find sameness were all my fault. Turns out, it's not a genetic anomaly, but just different genes." It was important that he understood. Since he'd seen that other side of her. In a work sense, his opinion of her mattered. And work was everything to her.

"How did you end things with your parents?" His question hit a bit hard, for a work situation. Mostly because that was the part where she was most lost.

"I hung up."

"You hung up on your parents." Jacob wasn't asking. Mae's straightforward words, the lift of her chin, the frank way she looked right at him as she made the admission left him in no doubt as to its authenticity.

She nodded. He wanted more. Almost pushed again. Remembered her tears the morning before. Knowing they'd prompted the discovery she'd just made, and ascertaining that she was doing better than she had been, he decided to leave well enough alone. For the time being.

He'd check back on the subject. But as long as she was doing okay for the moment, he had something more immediate on his mind.

"I don't think you should travel to and from work alone," he told her. "Or be anywhere but locked in your apartment alone, for that matter." His thoughts were becoming clearer and clearer on that one.

He'd solved the crime before it had happened. He couldn't just ignore the heads-up.

Eyes wide, and frowning at the same time, Mae said, "What on earth are you talking about? I'm not suicidal, Jacob. Not even close. I'm mad. I'm hurt. I'm probably in shock. But as you said, I'm also relieved. Going forward, my life might be much improved for knowing the truth about myself. It's just going to take a minute for me to catch up with the changed status."

Her tone of voice, the words, almost made him smile. With relief. For the first time since Saturday, he felt as though he was conversing with the woman he knew.

Following instincts that were growing steadily stronger, he said two words: "Ken Baylor."

Mae's head cocked, her gaze narrowed, sharpened, and in a professional tone he wholly recognized and admired, she asked, "What about him?"

"He's not only down three guys, the two kidnappers and Officer Olsen, but he knows that we have the bodies of the two victims and Olsen in our custody. With a gifted forensic scientist who has a state-of-the-art lab on-site. Meaning..."

"...finding the evidence to nail him quickly and efficiently," Mae finished his sentence, denoting total understanding, as was her way when they were working. "He won't have time to clean up shop." She nodded.

"Not with you well, present, and able to work. He's going to be getting more and more nervous, which means more desperate."

"You're as much of a target as I am."

His immediate head shake held frustration he didn't try to hide. "There are other ISB agents who can be here within hours. Beyond that, I'm trained to protect myself."

"I passed the self-defense training with flying colors."

"I carry a gun. You don't."

Jacob was surprised at the well of relief that flooded him when Mae nodded. He'd been gearing up for a fight with her. One he couldn't lose.

"For now, I'll drive you to and from work. You wait inside until I come up to get you. You don't leave on your own. If you need to get out, we'll arrange something. The department will cover delivery of anything you need. I'll have a camera installed on your front door with an alert on my phone. And someone on the outside of the building as well." He was planning on the fly.

And realizing that he couldn't get it all done that night, when Mae said, "For tonight, I'll spend the night here. It's not like I haven't done it countless times before."

She was right. And, as usual, his other half when it came to the business of solving crimes and protecting the innocent. He'd just never had a protectee quite so close to home before. Not personally.

Though, with the trafficking ring in town, his family was all on edge. Most particularly where his father, Sam, was concerned. Baylor's ex-wife, Susan, had not only been a neighbor, and friends with Kate, Jacob's mother, but Sam was dating her.

"I'll put the cot into the storage room if you want, and lock the door," Mae continued before he could respond. She waved a hand to a back corner of the lab, and he looked over at the cot that had been set up there almost as long as she'd been employed with ISB. She had a small, three-quarter bath in the lab, too. A shower, no tub.

One that other female law enforcement had used on occasion. There was a slightly larger similar setup for the male agents, with stalls.

And his decision was made. "I'll stay, too, tonight, just to be safe," he said. The couch in his office had been a bed to him countless times as well. He always kept a fresh uniform in his office. He got dirty a lot, working in the canyon wilderness. Didn't always have time to go home to shower and change.

They stood there, looking at each other, and Jacob asked, "Do you need to run to your place to pick up anything?" Mae usually kept spare clothes in the lab. There'd been more than one lab mishap requiring a new outfit. And when she was running tests, she absolutely wouldn't leave to clean up.

"No." She shook her head, and gave nothing else. Like she was waiting for something from him.

More that he should be saying? Or just wanting him to leave?

Not liking that he couldn't read her, when, until the past couple of days, doing so had been a given, Jacob left.

She hadn't had dinner, but Mae didn't feel particularly hungry, either. She had some fruit in the lab's refrigerator. And the vending room off the main hallway of the building had snacks if necessary.

Mostly, she was glad for an excuse to stay at the lab all night. She didn't so much fear Ken Baylor, though she definitely saw valid points in Jacob's theory that she could quickly become a target for the out-of-control former public official. Enough so that she was thankful for Jacob's offer of protection going forward.

At the moment, though, she was glad to be able to avoid going home. Or rather, happier to have reason to remain within the emotional and mental boundaries that being at work placed on her.

Hiding behind her work persona, perhaps. And so be it. If it got her through. Allowed her to stay focused so that she could be at her best over the next days and, God forbid, weeks, as they all worked together to end the cruelty being enacted upon the foster women in southern Utah.

To that end, she pulled out all the past five months' worth of evidence boxes pertaining to the kidnapping and human trafficking ring, intending to go through everything again, piece by piece, in case she'd missed something. Or, in light of more recent evidence, something had new significance.

Keeping her mind focused on a series of events that were far more weight bearing than her own birth discovery helped her find perspective, at least in the moment, and Mae gave her all to it. So much so that when Jacob came walking in the lab door more than an hour later, she almost dropped a test tube on the floor.

"What the..." She started to swear, at her own jumpiness, not the interruption, until she saw the pizza box in the man's hand.

From her favorite pizzeria. Not that hard for him to remember since it was his, too.

"Dinner is served, ma'am," he said, setting the box down on the smaller metal worktable perpendicular to her main one. He had napkins and soda cans from the vending machine, too. It wasn't their first working dinner. Or even their tenth.

But when it was just the two of them staying late, the meal, if there was one, was always shared in her lab.

Jacob didn't have the table space she did. And if she was there, it generally meant she had tests running. Which she'd need to monitor.

All was fine, normal, until she realized there was only one stool.

Because she'd purposely hidden his in the storage room. Not her best move. Not even a rational one.

And it wasn't a good time in her life for her to make either of those things known to the one man whose respect she didn't want to lose. Because of the current case. The work they had to do. They couldn't afford to be distracted.

"Here, take this stool," she said, moving it over to the smaller table, as the solution to her more personal dilemma hit her. "I needed the other one in the storage room and failed to bring it back out."

All true. And yet letting him draw his own conclusions as to why she'd had the other one in the storage closet.

"I told you to requisition a stepladder," he said, right on cue, and, back turned, on her way to undo her less-than-intelligent move of Monday morning, Mae smiled.

It was nice. Having dinner with Mae again. Being back on track. With the life he led, driven by crime every day, Jacob took the good moments where he could find them. In the past couple of years, and even more, the previous five months, he'd been finding more and more of them with Dr. Mae Copeland.

He didn't know what he'd do without her. A thought that had been occurring to him more and more of late. Had to be because of the case. So many young women. Some they'd probably never even know about. The more he learned, the more frantic he became to put an end to the reign of terror, and yet, even with all of the pieces they'd put together, he still couldn't nail the fiend his gut was sure was behind the entire enterprise.

Ken Baylor. The guy had always given him a bad vibe. A true narcissist if ever there was one. Handsome in the smarmiest of ways.

"We still have nothing that's going to get us a warrant on Baylor," Mae said, as she swallowed a bite of pizza. Ham and onion on her side. Deluxe on his. "I've tried on and off all day to figure out a way to prove that he used his public official connection to get those files from the foster system to track the women recently aging out who had no families. And I've failed."

Jacob nodded. He'd done the same. With like results. "You know my father's been seeing Ken's ex-wife?" he asked.

Mae nodded. "Sassy told me. She said he brought her to the silent auction that was held at her gallery a few months ago."

He nodded. Wishing he could leave it at that. And said, "It was to benefit the Colton Foundation," as though that would explain away the reason his father had chosen to show up with the woman on his arm. Telling the whole town that they were an item.

While Jacob was coming around to the idea that his

dad might have actually fallen in love again, in which case, he'd welcome the woman into their family willingly, he still struggled some with seeing his mother replaced. By the friend who'd helped nurse her through her illness.

"They share something sacred, you know," Mae said.

Her words snatched him out of his melancholy train of thought, but she'd lost him, too. "Who does?"

"Your dad and Susan Baylor. They both cared about your mom. And while the affection they felt for her was different, they both suffered from her loss. Just as the rest of your family did."

With a piece of pizza halfway to his mouth for a bite, Jacob stopped cold. One sentence, and something he'd been struggling with seemed to align itself right inside him. "Just as the rest of your family did." It was a bond they all shared. One that had drawn them closer.

And Susan wasn't an outsider to that. In a sense, she'd already been one of them before his father had started seeing her.

Which made what he had to do even harder. "I have to go talk to her about Ken." The weight had been bearing down on him all day.

The woman had been victimized by the man through her marriage, with his cheating while she was at home nursing their terminally ill son. By his jealousy of all the attention she'd given to the boy. And he'd continued to torment her after the divorce, too. Even using his connections to discredit her catering business.

Mae knew as much about all of that as Jacob did. It had come up on a dossier he'd run. With other corroborating details being provided by the local and state law enforcement.

"She'll understand," Mae said. Then, added, "It might even help her, you know, to be able to actually do something to stop Ken from terrorizing others. It could help her heal."

Not a way his thoughts would have traveled.

But as had become the case more often than not, Mae's perspective enhanced his own in a way that made life more palatable.

And he was glad that they were back to normal.

Chapter 7

Mae didn't want Jacob to leave. That night, in the lab, after work time, without new evidence pushing at her, took on an aura of time out of time as she sat there eating pizza. Like those moments wouldn't have any effect on real life one way or the other.

She talked to him about the evidence she was looking at again. They discussed a few possibilities she'd explore. And then she said, "Sassy did my hair and makeup the other day. She chose the dress, too." Something that, the more she'd thought about, the more she'd wanted him to know.

It had been his first time out in a social situation with her. She didn't want him to think she was two dichotomous people in one body.

When he nodded, showing no surprise whatsoever that his cousin had helped her, she rolled her eyes and gave a self-deprecatory grin. "She told you."

"Yeah. Just because she knows we work closely together. She wanted me to know."

Knowing Sassy, Mae wasn't sure that was exactly how it had gone. Or that Sassy's motives had been informational only, but because she wasn't willing to risk walking into any kind of an uncomfortable situation that put her and Jacob at odds again, she let it go.

If his cousin knew that Jacob had been with Mae the previous Saturday night, and had been in any way teasing him, or inferring that there was something between them, it was none of Mae's business.

He'd deal with it.

"She didn't know I was your plus-one," Jacob said then, in between bites.

And she had to ask. "Does she now?"

"Nope."

At that news, Mae helped herself to another piece of pizza.

So much of the time she and Jacob were on the same wavelength. A pleasantry she was no longer so sure she had to give up now that she knew she wasn't so much awkward as just differently comprised from the rest of her family. And because she'd been designed for something unlike the people who'd raised her, that didn't mean there was anything wrong with her.

Thoughts came and went.

But by the time the pizza was gone, Mae was feeling a whole lot better than she had since the wedding.

Jacob was tired. In some ways, exhausted even, but as he cleaned up the pizza trash, he wasn't ready to head to his office, to sit alone.

Didn't make much sense, him feeling that way. He sat alone every single night at his condo just a few blocks away. And his office was more of a home to him than the place where he slept. He spent a hell of a lot more time at the ISB building than he did in his residence.

Besides… Mae was showing signs of feeling better. He wanted to think that he'd had something to do with that.

And he was enjoying her company. He'd only been without it for two days, and yet, he'd missed their conversations.

He just didn't want to talk about work. Which wasn't their norm. But they'd been enmeshed in unending dark tragedy for five months straight. It was the longest case he'd ever been the lead on and it was taking its toll.

Not that he'd admit that to Mae. Or anyone else.

"I ran into Chay when I went next door to pick up the pizza," he shared what came to mind. Not usual for them, but it felt okay. He'd met her family. He could talk about his.

Mae was leaning forward with her arms on the table, seemingly fine to sit a while, as she asked, "Did he have some news for us?" The Navajo Tribal Affairs officer had been a part of the trafficking case since twenty-five-year-old former foster child Fern Hensley, a kidnapping victim on the way to being sold into human trafficking, had been rescued from a burning shack located on the reservation.

Made sense Mae would think he was bringing up the officer because of the case. Why else? Except, there he was, doing it. Shaking his head, he said, "Nope. He actually stopped to tell me he was my cousin-in-law." He raised his brows, watching her, half nodded. Not really sure what to do with himself in the foreign territory into which he'd wandered. "He and Ava got married at the courthouse so they can legally adopt Ella Grace sooner."

"Wow!" Her smile, the light in Mae's brown eyes, was

just what he'd needed. And had a feeling Mae was benefiting from the happier topic as well. "How's your family going to take not getting an invitation to the wedding?"

He grinned again. "Oh, there's going to be one. Chay was quick to point that out. My guess is probably by the end of the summer. They just wanted to wait until after the baby is legally theirs and truly settled."

Mae's smile was softer than he was used to seeing as she said, "So there's a happy ending in this god-awful case."

The baby's mother, Annie, had died at the hands of the kidnappers. Because she'd seen her roommate, and co-caregiver for the baby, be pulled into a black van.

One of the missing women who hadn't yet been found.

Jacob hadn't meant to fall right back into the dark side. Except that it was pretty much all he could think about. How could he not when it was up to him to stop the man at the top from feeding his greed in such an obscene way.

Every second Jacob took his mind off the case was one second more of agony for young women who needed him to find them. Or protect them from being the next in a long line of unknowns who'd disappeared.

"We have to stop him before he packs up shop and moves to some other area where he can schmooze his way into their foster records, target his prey, and start all over."

Mae's hand fell on the table between them. Almost as though she was reaching out to him. "You're pulling this all together, Jacob. Working so well with all the other law enforcement departments, even tribal police, managing to piece so much together, you're pulling off a miracle here. We're at the last piece. The top dog. We've got him.

We just have to find a way to prove it in a manner that will stand up in court. Then we get names and dates out of him. And go find those girls."

Some of them. Jacob knew that some of them would never be found. But as he met and held Mae's gaze, the strength shining from her eyes seemed to beam clear through to his soul. They were going to stop future travesties for the unsuspecting young women just trying to live their lives.

And they'd find some of those who'd already been trapped.

Mae believed that.

Which helped Jacob believe, too.

Mae slept better that night than she'd expected. Better than she had in a long time. Odd, in that she'd had such shocking news, and yet, while she couldn't quite wrap her mind around the fact that her parents weren't biologically hers, she wasn't biologically theirs, and that she was biologically linked to two strangers, she felt more like herself than she ever had before.

She understood. Logically.

She wasn't so much a misfit, maladjusted, as she was just different from the farm family in which she'd been raised. It wasn't something wrong with her. Or with them, either, though she'd always taken the brunt of the blame on herself.

And the time spent with Jacob had relaxed her, too. Normalized her. More so because her bombshell had taken away the sense of vulnerability she'd felt around him after the wedding. The pat on the back, the kid gloves, had been a result of his own awkward attempt to step outside his comfort zone to make sure she was okay.

An emotional version of the pizza he'd brought for dinner that night.

They'd merely proved something they both already knew. Neither one of them did the mushy stuff well. Which was what allowed them to stay focused when the evidence in front of them was filled with horrors. The world needed people like them, ones who could sit with the worst of the worst as long as it took to find and obliterate the source. Without them, evil would be allowed to prevail.

In gray pants and a black T-shirt, with her hair up in a black clip, and her white lab coat on, Mae pulled her stool from the small to the large silver metal table just after dawn Wednesday morning with renewed vigor.

Ordinarily, after a night at work, which would have meant catching an hour or two of sleep in between checking her machines, analyzing results, starting tests accordingly, she'd head out to drive through for some fast-food breakfast and coffee, bringing it back to the lab. But with Jacob's Ken Baylor warning ringing with complete truth in her mind, she texted the agent instead. Placed an order.

And got to work until breakfast arrived. She'd had an epiphany in the shower that morning and was eager to talk to her counterpart about it.

Which she did before she'd even opened the foam container that Jacob placed on her little table less than twenty minutes later. He hadn't brought any for himself. Just dropped and turned to go.

"I have a suggestion for you," she said to his departing back.

His instant turn, the raised brows and openness in his expression did her heart good. "Susan Baylor. Call your dad. Find out a time when he and Susan are going to be together. Plan with him that you'll drop by. And talk to her with him present." She believed it's what he would have done if it was his mother he had to question.

For many reasons. "That way you don't tip off her ex that you're interrogating her. You allow her to feel more like a family member, like she's helping you out. With your father there, she'll be more comfortable. All of which will get you more from her than if you question her officially, which would put up natural defenses even if she didn't mean it to happen."

He was staring at her. His chin tight, lips pursed. And she said, "And it will help you out with your father, too. Allowing him to be there to protect his girlfriend, so to speak. To comfort her in what will surely be a difficult conversation. A woman who's come out of an abusive marriage carries the scars for the rest of her life, no matter how happy she might currently be."

She was speaking from years of examining evidence, on that one. Of reading case files.

And she was overstepping her boundaries with Jacob. But they were in new territory. His needing to take the case into a personal venue to get to a key witness. A woman he struggled to accept as his father's love interest partially because she'd been friends with Jacob's mother.

And a case that was the biggest either she or Jacob had ever had before them.

"Maybe you should come along."

At first, she thought he was being sarcastic. His way of telling her she'd overstepped her job description. A first between them, granted, but…seriously. "Why on earth would I do that?"

"Because you can explain evidence to her better than I can. She's going to have questions. I know her well enough to know that. And if, as you say, she's carrying underlying scars from her ex-husband's abuse, it will help her to have another woman present. And help the case to have that woman be one who's as knowledgeable about and as focused on getting results as I am."

It was a lot for him. She wasn't sure what to do with it. Logically he made sense. Good sense. But…the two of them…*her*…physically present during an interrogation, not just listening over Wi-Fi in her lab as she'd done on occasion…she wasn't sure…had no experience in that area…didn't want to hurt the case.

"We have to get this guy, Mae," Jacob said. "Susan's our best shot at doing so in a way that will hold up in court. And, as you rightly pointed out, I'm adjusting to the woman's role in my father's life. I have no doubt as to my ability to get this done. Your insights show me that we have a better shot of getting the most possible information from her if we both go."

She nodded. Glanced at the yellow foam that contained her breakfast. Wasn't sure she wanted it. "Let me know when," she said, and then turned her back on him, on food and coffee, and focused on the evidence over which she had complete control.

Sam Colton responded to Jacob's text immediately. He and Susan were on the reservation, helping to harvest greens and herbs at the community gardens. A project started by local government to help tribal families live healthier lives.

Jacob and Mae met them there, in a small private room Chay provided for them in one of the official buildings. But only after Jacob drove around long enough to make certain they weren't being followed.

And Chay did a thorough check of the surroundings. The Navajo tribal officer was going to be watching surveillance cameras in the area during the meeting as well.

Susan and Mae were not going to be placed further at risk for helping to put a deranged man away.

Jacob's lawyer father, still straight, tall, and trim at sixty-one, ran a hand through his thick salt-and-pepper hair as he stood when Chay showed Jacob and Mae into the room. His dark brown gaze sought his son's immediately, and Jacob held it with confidence and respect. He didn't have to say a word for his dad to know that dragging Susan into her ex-husband's deviant activities was a last resort.

Susan, two years younger than Sam, a caterer and thin but healthy looking, remained seated. Unlike Jacob and Mae, who'd not only showered at ISB that morning but were dressed for work, the older two were in shorts, tank tops, and tennis shoes.

As Jacob and Mae sat side by side on another small couch across from Sam and Susan, Jacob noticed the long look his father gave Mae. He had no idea what his father was thinking. And didn't want to know.

He turned his gaze to Susan. And with Mae's words in mind, said, "First, Susan, thank you so much for this. I'm sorry I even have to ask. Trust me, if I saw any way other than dragging you into this mess, I would take it."

Her bright blue eyes met his gaze straight on as she nodded, her blond bob like a light around her head. "I'd already talked to your dad about helping in any way I could. As soon as he warned me that it looked like Ken might be involved."

She clasped her hands together then, her thumbs doing circles around each other, and he felt Mae shift beside him. Looking at his forensic scientist, he gave her a nod.

"I've been going through what look to be some of Ken's files. They contain records of older foster children. All female," she started in. "Was there ever a time the two of you were considering adopting a daughter?"

Eyes wide, Susan gave a "No" that was short and to the point. Punctuated by a "Never."

And Jacob asked, "Do you know of any reason why he'd have had the records?"

"Not a legal one." Susan seemed to shrink a bit.

Jacob noticed his father's hand slide gently over to cover Susan's thigh. An intimate move. Meant to show her she was no longer attached to the nasty human being, Jacob figured. To let her know that she had the love of a good man.

Not a case-related thought. But not one that brought negative vibes from within him, either.

"You believe your ex-husband is capable of selling these women, don't you?" Mae's soft question came from beside Jacob. And the older woman nodded.

Looking more angry than afraid. Kudos to Mae.

And he got to his point. Wanting to make the interrogation as quick and painless for her as possible. "I need to know if you can think of anything that could help point us to anyplace, anything, anyone that Ken might access to pull off a successful ongoing ring of kidnapping and then trafficking these women. People who might feel that they owe him, who'd be willing to carry out any of the duties he'd need done. Kidnapping. Transporting. Housing. Buying."

"The smallest memory could help," Mae said then. "I was just recently able to pinpoint a three-mile radius outside of Dark Canyon where one of the kidnapped women had been at some point, just by a leaf. Seriously, anything. A color of mud you might have seen on a boot at some point. Or maybe on a pair of dress shoes. At a time when he'd been in a suit, maybe, and you'd thought he'd been at his office in the public building all day."

The woman frowned, clearly looking inward, but shook her head slowly. Then stopped. "Anyplace, you said." Her glance included both him and Mae. And, in unison, they nodded.

"He used to have this old house someplace in the Dark Canyon Wilderness. Said he bought it off a guy who was going into foreclosure. He thought we could remodel it together and use it as a getaway from the city. I later learned that he rented it out to help finance his first political campaign."

Mae wasn't moving. Jacob asked, "Do you have an address? Even a general location?"

Susan shook her head. "I just know that he told me that the government needed the land for other purposes. He called the purchase of a home on parkland inholding. Said the government could take the property and home at any time, they just had to compensate him for it. Which he said they did. But I later heard someone say that they'd heard that he'd put the place up for rent again.

This was a few years ago. But it was after he'd told me he no longer owned the place."

"He probably didn't want to have to pay you half its value in the divorce," Jacob said. He'd handled enough domestic violence cases to know those ropes.

"Or to have you claim half of the income from it," Sam added.

Susan looked between them. "It wasn't in his name," she said. "He couldn't donate any more to his own campaign."

"What name was it in?" Jacob's question was a little too sharp. Something he noticed after it was too late to compensate.

"I have no idea."

Mae had been rapidly thumb-typing on her phone. And scrolling. Then asked, "Have you ever seen photos of the property?"

Susan nodded. "When he first purchased it and wanted me to help him remodel it."

Standing to approach the woman, she handed Susan her phone. "Are any of these it?"

The older woman scrolled, studied, then handed the phone back, shaking her head. "It was brick. One story. Front door right in the middle. No garage. I remember because in the photo I saw an old car, a tiller, a bike, rakes and shovels, and some kind of trellis thing all just on the side of the house."

Jacob sat forward. "What about a driveway?"

"There was one," Susan said. "But it wasn't paved. It wasn't just tire tracks, either. It was like a dirt road almost leading to it."

A house at the end of a dirt road. In the Dark Canyon Wilderness. That had been purchased from another private holder. He was on his way. “Any idea how long ago he bought it?”

Shaking her head, Susan frowned, then said, “It was about a year before our son, Andrew, died. I remember because he wanted me to help him renovate it, but I couldn’t leave Andrew at that point and Ken got mad. Said that he deserved some of my time, too.”

Jacob was ready to go. He had enough without putting Susan through any more. Death records would show him a year in which to start his search. From there private holdings on parkland would narrow down his search considerably, and if there were no photos, he’d send officers to check out every single one of them until he found the place.

Standing, he approached Susan, who, with Sam, also stood. He held out his hand, intending to shake hers, but it was as though Mae, somewhere behind him, was pushing at his back. She wasn’t. At all. And still, he could feel Mae’s presence as he leaned forward, loping the arm he’d held out around the older woman’s shoulders to give her a little side squeeze.

It was nothing like the hug he’d have given his mother.

But it was a start.

Chapter 8

Officer Chayton Benally, Jacob's friend and colleague, met them in the hall not far from the room where they'd been with Susan and Sam. Mae knew the man, but not well.

He smiled at her, though, included her in his glance as he asked how the interview went, and as soon as Jacob told him about the house Ken Baylor had owned, the tribal cop took them to his office, where the three of them stood around his keyboard, looking at his computer screen.

"I've already looked at Dark Canyon title records for parkland," Mae said. "We need to go farther out than that. She said she saw a tiller, and what sounded like other gardening tools, a trellis, which would mean ground that was being used to grow something. Probably food. Maybe not. But either way, it's going to be in an area where the ground is softer, unlike most of this area, where it's all rocky."

Both men looked at her, nodded, and Chay started to type.

Fifteen minutes later, address in hand, Jacob knocked his friend on the shoulder, told him to watch his back, and followed closely behind Mae as they headed out to his car.

He was so close she could feel his body heat. Mae didn't take it personally. She knew he was just doing his job.

Her flesh didn't understand the nuances. It tingled, and started to heat her insides inappropriately. To the point of sending a message to her brain that sent a vision to her consciousness of the fly portion of the man's green work pants.

She'd noticed it before, of course. She was single, not dead. Celibate by choice, not because she didn't experience bouts of sexual desire.

But that morning the sensation was amplified beyond an immediate dismissal. It lingered even after she was buckled in the passenger side of his SUV. And could have become a concern if not for the fact that they were on the hunt for a horrific man.

And had a viable lead.

"It was good, having you back there," Jacob said as, his navigation set, he pushed his hands-free button to make a call. And then, before she could respond, he was telling his car's phone system to call the office. From there, he requested an agent to collect a local law enforcement officer in the jurisdiction of the house, and meet them at the residence.

And then called a judge he knew at the local courthouse for a warrant.

In the hour it took them to arrive at the unkempt residence out in the country on an outcropping of parkland, his request for the right to enter the premise, to search it, had come through to the ISB office. And to Jacob's phone.

They were first to arrive. Mae's heart pounded as Jacob slowed at the drive where navigation told them to turn.

"Someone's been here recently," she said aloud. "But not in the past week or so." She could tell by the growth already filling in tire tracks in the weeds growing at the turn in.

"Could have been someone turning around," Jacob said, his gaze intent as he took in the area. Heart pounding, Mae wasn't sure she should have come along. She wasn't a field officer.

But at the thought of possibly seeing Ken Baylor's evidence firsthand, at having the opportunity to be the first one to access it, she knew she had to keep her fears to herself, master them, and focus on the work.

"Get down," Jacob told her then. "I'm going to circle the place, and in case I scare up something for which we aren't prepared, I want you out of the line of fire."

She did as she was told. But said, "There's no evidence of habitation since those weeds were knocked down," she told him. Then added, "Look at the handle on the front door. The dust storm that came through a couple of days ago would have left residue on it." She'd spent the drive researching what she could of the area. Preparing herself.

Keeping her mind in scientific territory. Immersing herself as deeply as possible so that she'd be able to recognize and conclude at first sight. As she had with the recent weed death and partial regrowth.

And then, sitting on the floor of the front seat, looking up at him, said, "What happens if you get shot?"

"I won't."

He didn't know that. He wasn't superhuman.

But she believed him.

Parking his SUV well behind the house, in a ditch that kept it from being visible from the road or the drive, Jacob told Mae to stay put until he could check out the house. And then, once he was as convinced as she was that there was no one in the immediate vicinity, he escorted her quickly from the vehicle to the back door of the place.

When he tried the knob, found the door locked, he kicked it in.

And stood right beside her as they each took one step in and stopped. A single wooden chair was mounted to the floor with metal plates, where a kitchen table might once have been.

"The chains," Mae said, her tone low, filled with notes he recognized. Anger and determination. The two forces that drove her to find every answer he needed. She was already approaching the chair. "They're the same shape." Pulling out her phone, she brought up an app, held the phone's screen to the chain, and said, "Three-eighths inch, calibrated, just like the measurements I took off Maura Bennet."

Holding up her phone, she started to snap numerous photos, from all angles of the chain. As though the stuff was the only piece of evidence in the place.

But he got it. As a whole, she'd be overwhelmed.

One piece at a time, she was in control.

And that was how they, and the rangers who arrived,

handled every inch of the small old house that day. It took them hours to photograph, tag, bag, and box.

They'd found what had to be a transition house. Titled in the name of a cop who'd trained under Olsen years ago. And had been dead for more than a year.

With no family to claim the home that Ken Baylor had paid for and used. Jacob still had no viable proof with which to arrest the former lieutenant governor. The man was so greasy he'd ruled in such a way that all of the bad deeds slid right off him.

For the moment.

Piece by piece, Jacob's multidepartment team was getting one hell of a lot closer.

The blood alone was going to keep Mae busy for more hours than the day held. She'd collected samples from all over the house. From walls, the floor, the chains. The chair. And in the bathroom, too. She had no idea how many different types, representing how many different people, she was going to find.

Wasn't even sure what she should hope for. One or two people who'd been brutalized so badly they were dead?

Or a number of them who'd bled in that house and then moved on.

If she was lucky, she'd get a male DNA match among them. And hopefully that would be the final nail in Ken Baylor's coffin.

And that was just the blood. Jacob dropped her at the back door of the ISB building, shielding her with the car as she slipped inside. And then carried down box after box from the back of his SUV to her lab. Stacking them on a counter that ran the whole length of a sidewall.

They'd found fingernails, empty water bottles. Syringes, but no drugs. Clothing. Even a package of crackers in the cupboard. But no cameras or photos. With the digital age, Mae hadn't expected to find either.

"I'm going to stay and help you document all this," Jacob told her. As the lead on the case, he called the shots. But she agreed with the call.

"You'll get a firsthand look at it all so you know what you have. And I can get to work testing each thing one by one, finding the significance of each, so you can build your case," she told him. As though he didn't know exactly why he'd made the choice.

Or maybe it was because he had other reasons for sticking close to her and she didn't want to deal with any of that, so she was telling him why she wasn't fighting the decision.

At least one person had been tied up. She was getting epithelial evidence from ropes found on the floor. Based on the blood, they'd been roughed up pretty badly.

She and the rangers, including a crime scene investigator, had taken enough dried fluid samples to keep Mae busy for a month. She didn't have a week to get through them all. She started tests running within five minutes of having arrived back at her lab.

Preparing herself for the depth of degradation she was going to find.

Jacob had driven through for sandwiches for them on the way to the transition house. She'd eaten half of one and that had taxed her stomach.

She was no hungrier when six o'clock hit and Jacob asked what she wanted him to order in for dinner.

Her mumbled reply of "Nothing" wasn't going to fly.

Not even her own logical mind could deny the need for food. She had to eat or she'd be less effective. Shc wanted an Indian taco. Fry bread. With ground beef, beans, lettuce, tomatoes, and sour cream. Nothing else. No salsa. None of the jalapenos she usually popped like candy.

And though he cocked a brow at her choice, Jacob didn't argue with her.

Which warmed Mae's frozen heart a little.

With just a hint of an idea of the atrocities that had taken place in Ken Baylor's transition house, Jacob was more on edge than he cared to admit as he carried dinner into his office and went down to the lab to get Mae. He needed her there, working, and he had to get her out of there, too, at least to breathe air that didn't contain the copious amounts of pain and suffering that were so overwhelming even he was struggling to harden himself against it.

He couldn't take her out of the building, not without ramping up his danger radar, and with others still there working late on the case, he couldn't ask her to dine in the break room, either. The last thing the introvert needed was a roomful of people asking questions, relying on her for the answers they didn't have the ability to find through research.

It was a testimony to the case that he'd spent the entire trip to Mae's lab analyzing his reasons for them having dinner in his office. A private place that no one entered when his door was shut.

He was bothered. Bad.

As, apparently, was she as she didn't even frown when he asked if she was in a place where she could leave just long enough to eat. "I just need a few minutes, and I'll be there," she told him.

He waited fifteen. Was just getting ready to go find her when she walked into his office.

"Shut the door," he told her. Pulling the food out of the warming bag it had come in and putting her container on the far side of his desk while he sat behind it.

They ate in silence. As though by joint decision. Jacob couldn't speak for Mae, but he was grateful for the quiet. With her there.

As though she was somehow reassuring him that they'd get the work done, just by being in his space.

He hoped she believed they'd get Baylor before he had a chance to kidnap another young woman. Thinking otherwise would make the work she was doing so much harder to bear.

Seeing the test results, reading what the evidence was telling her… He'd much rather have a gun pointed at his head. That was something he knew how to deal with.

Halfway through her flatbread, she pulled out her phone. Looked at it. Blinked and set it, face down beside her paper plate on his desk.

Her expression was placid, but he'd seen a flash of something different. Reminding him of the wedding he'd attended with her. "Have you talked to your parents?" he asked her.

It wasn't like she'd had any free time that day, but he'd had to ask. It would be inhumane to pretend that her world hadn't just been upended.

She shook her head. Then, instead of changing the subject as he'd expected, she said, "They've all texted me. My brothers, once each. Mom and Dad multiple times."

He glanced at her phone. "And that was one of them again?"

"Mom," she said, then took a bite of her big round taco as though it was any other day.

"And you haven't responded?"

She shook her head.

Jacob ate a couple of bites. Mae's personal situation was out of his jurisdiction. Totally. And yet, there he was, with a head full of things to say to her about it. He compromised with just one. "You should at least let them know you're okay," he told her. "You live alone. And there's a kidnapper on the loose."

"They don't know that."

He couldn't let that one go. "With Victor Olsen's arrest, everyone knows it." Women in a hundred-mile radius had been warned to be on the alert. By every means possible.

"They don't watch the news."

He watched her take another bite. Avoiding his gaze. "Mae." His tone was firm. "They go to town. Talk to people. Your brothers' wives have family..."

She cut him off with the wave of her hand. Looked up at him. "I know," she said. "I just don't know what to say to them."

That one seemed obvious to him. "Maybe just that you're okay, but need some time?"

She held his gaze. Nodded. And he added, "You don't have to tackle the situation all at once."

Picking up her phone, Mae tapped and typed, then tapped some more. Then, back at her lettuce and tomato flatbread taco, said, "I did a group message to all four of them," and took another bite of her dinner.

Jacob sat back. Feeling oddly better.

Maybe just because, for a few minutes, they hadn't been dealing with blood and death and stolen lives.

But he didn't think so.

Jacob had been right. She didn't have to take on the whole of a situation and expect to solve all of the pieces in one fell swoop. She shouldn't have needed the reminder.

But was grateful to him for providing it just the same.

Finished with her meal, she sat back, a can of soda in hand, and said, "Thank you."

"No problem. The department paid for it."

If she'd been more herself she might have rolled her eyes at that one. Except that, in any normal day—normal for before, she wasn't sure what normal in the future was going to look like—she wouldn't have issued the gratitude aloud at all.

She and Jacob had never had to bother with the niceties. They'd just always seemed to understand that they were there between them. Always. Unspoken, but…felt.

"I meant for reminding me that in order to solve a problem, you have to take it piece by piece. I, as much as anyone, know that. This thing with my family… I have no idea how I feel. Or rather, I feel so many warring things that I don't even know what I want right now. So I can't possibly figure out how to go about making it happen."

It wasn't his business.

"Do you love them?" he asked.

"Of course. Biology doesn't change that."

"Coming from a large, close-knit family, I can tell you this. You start with that. Love, and being a unit.

The history. And take whatever time you need to figure out the rest."

She'd held his gaze steadily the whole time he was talking. Gaining a measure of relief from his words, as he said, "I get upset with my brothers on a regular basis." He shook his head. "And they get on my nerves half the time, too. Mostly because they try to. But I count on them and they count on me." He shrugged. Then added, "My life would never be the same without them."

The words hit home. With a power that truly did settle a bit of the battle raging within Mae.

And with that, she bundled up her trash, and his, and left him sitting there.

Chapter 9

Jacob needed Baylor's prints inside that house. Hell, he'd settle for some anywhere on the property. The longer the man was out there, the more endangered the women in the area would become. One thing Jacob knew, a man who so carefully planned and carried out the running of an intricate human trafficking ring didn't do it just for the money.

Baylor needed the feeling of control over women, for starters. Jacob couldn't lose himself getting into the man's head, beyond that. Didn't want to understand how a man could be driven to send young women off into purgatory for any reason. Let alone take some kind of positive affirmation from doing so.

The need to control females, though, that chilled Jacob's blood. Even if he stopped the former public official's human trafficking ring, if he didn't get Baylor himself, the man would find another way to torment women. Jacob would bet his life on that one.

He and Mae weren't the only ones working late that night. Chay was on the reservation going through all camera footage within five miles of the transition house, dating back six months and forward. Local deputies who had jurisdiction of the area immediately outside the perimeter of parkland where the house was located were combing the area on foot, still, gathering everything, even a twig if it looked as though it might have been touched. And canvassing every home and business within a two-mile radius, too, asking if anyone had seen anything, or knew anything about the comings and goings at the house. They were also asking for private home and business camera footage and were sending it along to Chay as they obtained it.

With Officer Victor Olsen's recent arrest in Wilson, Jacob was a little leery of county deputies that he didn't know personally on the case. And had a couple of rangers assisting them, ostensibly only to be extra hands. Just in case.

Jacob had already put in a request for national government aerial footage. As an ISB agent, as opposed to a park ranger, he was officially stationed out of Washington and had contacts there. Impatiently awaiting the red tape requirements to be completed, intending to go through that footage himself, he took a few-minute break while others were still in the building to run by his condo for a few things. And to grab a couple of items from Mae's place, too.

And while, since he was doing his run, he'd offered to make the stop, and had been relieved when Mae hadn't argued with him about her need to stay out of sight as much as possible, he hadn't fully contemplated the actual carrying out of the endeavor. He knew where she lived. Had been by the place countless times. Had even stopped in front of the apartment building as recently as the past weekend when he drove her to and from her cousin's wedding.

He'd never been inside before.

The second he stepped in the door he'd just unlocked

with the key she'd given him from her ring, he was a different man. It was like he'd entered another realm. A world where he was someone else. A guy who breathed in auras. One who could have an elemental connection to a woman. One woman.

It was nonsense, of course. The day had been long and incredibly harsh. On so many levels. Professionally and personally.

Talking to Susan, seeing his father's hand slide gently on the other woman's thigh… He'd seen a part of being a man that he'd never experienced. A simple touch. That did so much.

And Mae…everywhere. All over. The interrogation, the crime scene. Her shocking biological truth. The women…the god-awful number of young women…that he hadn't yet avenged. Those he hadn't yet saved as long as Ken Baylor was still free, walking among them.

It was no wonder he'd have a moment. He was human. Not a machine.

Mae's home was small. Three rooms. But they were laid out with spaciousness in mind. And, noticing the pull-down faucet in the kitchen, the cooking island, he was glad to see that she'd at least chosen a place with some luxuries. The woman spent every waking hour serving the world, people she'd never met. It pleased him to see that she at least allowed herself a few nice things in life.

He was there for a box of the fiber bars she bought in bulk and brought, one at a time, to her lab. And for a change of clothes.

She'd told him where to locate what she wanted. Bottoms and tops, all hanging together in the closet. The summer ones on the left. Any pants, any short-sleeved shirt. Just a couple of each. She had a stackable laundry unit in the lab for spills and contaminations.

He picked three out of the nine or ten pairs hanging there. So she wouldn't have to do laundry. He'd like to believe that it was overkill. That Baylor would be in custody within the next twenty-four hours, but he wasn't sure.

Another fact that was eating at him.

He was good at what he did. He should be. It was all he did.

So how did one sixty-two-year-old, smarmy ex-everything with little power or money manage to elude him over and over again, for five long months?

Grabbing three short-sleeved shirts that matched the pants, Jacob hung them on the doorknob, evading more than a cursory glance at the bed so he didn't trip over it, and focused on the long dresser across from it.

It was queen-size. The bed he wasn't looking at. With a lot of pillows. All gray. The pillows. The comforter was black.

Black and white. Mae. Shades of gray. The world in which she lived.

He needed the top drawer on the left. Pulled. Grabbed a handful of undergarments, and shoved them in his shirt pockets. Then, snatching up the hangers from the door, fled the room. And the apartment.

Like he was some kind of foreign object being thrust from an ejector. With the bulges at his chest, he sure as hell felt like one.

It wasn't as though he hadn't seen undergarments before. He walked by them at the big-box store every time he had to get to the men's section.

When his mom had been sick, he'd done laundry to help out his dad more than once.

He'd been with probably more than his share of women, too.

Bras and panties were just pieces of clothing. He had no idea if Mae's were even sexy or not. Judging by her normal apparel, they were probably just serviceable pieces of…silk.

They weren't cotton. He'd touched them.

He'd have thought cotton.

He shouldn't be thinking about them at all. And yet, as he climbed back into his truck and pulled the offenders away from his shirt, shoving them into the pockets of the pants they accompanied—as he'd done earlier with his own change of clothes—all he could think about was that silk.

Over and over again.

Yeah, Mae had a body. Okay, a very nice one. He'd be dead if he hadn't noticed. But it wasn't in his jurisdiction. And no slips of silk were going to change that.

Period.

Mae didn't see Jacob again that night. She'd expected to. Had counted on it, actually, since he'd been bringing her fresh clothes. But he'd been called out on a potential new victim. A recently aged-out foster female in Page, Arizona, three hours away, hadn't shown up for work for two days. And wasn't answering her phone.

Jacob had issued a be-on-the-lookout order to all law enforcement on the edges of the Navajo reservation and had gotten the call on his way back with her change of clothes. He'd left them in his office for her to pick up.

Not wanting to take anyone off their current jobs working the transition house, he'd decided to go to Page himself.

And had been in touch with Mae—and others—keeping apprised of their progress during his drive. She'd talked to him four times by the time she was dropping down to her cot for a few hours of sleep. Twice her call, twice his, and all about the evidence she was going through in her lab. She hadn't even pulled up the blanket, let alone closed her eyes, when her phone rang again.

"I'm headed back," Jacob told her, and feeling a bit of tension leave her body, she lay back, staring through the shadows at the ceiling. She was fine without him there. Had enough work to keep her occupied, without sleep, for the next few days.

She'd just grown used to having him around.

"Did they find her?" she asked. He wouldn't have left, otherwise.

"Yeah."

Tensing again, she asked, "Alive?" And wondered about the evidence.

"She's unconscious. Beaten up. But doesn't fit our case. Melanie Heath was dumped on the reservation, probably left to die, like Annie, but it's looking more like a boyfriend. He's currently missing. Showed up for work today, but left early. He had some bruising on his hand and scratch marks on his neck. Said the neck came from his cat. Didn't explain the bruising. Just went out for lunch and never came back."

"Did you see her?"

"Briefly." He sounded tired. Maybe more than she'd ever heard him. It was hard to tell. With her personal business hitting her during the worst case of her life, she was teetering on a bout of exhaustion herself.

"There were no chain marks, or any indication that

she'd been tied up," he continued. "And he'd beaten up her face pretty bad."

It wasn't part of their case. Mae was relieved. And then, thinking about the woman who had to face the future running from a man she'd trusted, or testifying against him court, if she was lucky, she felt bad again.

Still, "It's better for her that she wasn't hauled off and sold across the border," she concluded aloud. Had she been one of Baylor's victims, the woman's face would have been left in pristine condition.

Jacob didn't respond, and she had a quick flash of fear at the thought that he was falling asleep at the wheel. "Jacob?"

"Yeah, I'm here. Just taking a sip of coffee."

Okay. Good. "You've been at it over eighteen hours and it was a pretty crap day. You should stop and get some sleep. This will all still be here in the morning." It wasn't like she hadn't spent the night alone in the building before.

Many times. More without anyone else even knowing she was doing so. When evidence called her, she answered.

"I'll be fine," he told her. "With everyone else leaving for the night, Chay's bunking down in my office, just until I get there. Then he's heading here. With the girl's body being found on the reservation, he's going to do the follow-up."

She didn't want to feel relieved to know that Officer Benally was still in the building. But her logical wants and emotional feelings had been at war ever since the damned wedding. How could one mistake in judgment ricochet so drastically?

She didn't have time to waste energy on something she couldn't change. Going forward, she'd be more aware of the damage her emotions could do if they weren't tended to properly. They were a biological part of her, just like everything else.

They deserved their due. And would take it even if she didn't grant it to them.

And right then, they were expressing concern over Jacob's long trip home over road that traveled through mostly deserted mountain and desert land. With few gas stations to provide coffee stops.

"I've got a thermos of coffee to keep me company, compliments of the Page police," Jacob said then, almost as though he could read her mind.

Which, he could. She could generally tell what he was thinking, too. When it came to work, at any rate.

But it wasn't her thoughts that were prompting her as she got off the cot, made herself a pot of coffee, and took the first cup back to her makeshift bed.

It wasn't like she and Jacob had nothing to talk about. With all of the results she'd gotten in the past few hours, they'd be focused until he was back in his office.

Starting with, "They need to check her for drugs." And then added, "I got positive confirmation that the same drug found in Annie and Fern was used on Maura Bennet." She named the specific combination. A common sedative used in date crimes. "While the face beating doesn't fit, Baylor's likely working with new hires. Something went wrong, they got violent and bailed. Leaving her for dead. And if that's the case..."

"... I left my information at the hospital," Jacob interrupted.

He'd already covered the base. She was glad to hear it. Glad to know that one of them, at least, was still in top form.

* * *

Jacob buzzed with alertness, driving over the dark roads into nothingness for as far as he could see. The coffee helped. Mae's conversation far more so.

Right or wrong, he allowed himself to partake of her unspoken offer for company to get him home safely. He was tired. So was she. They both had long days ahead of them.

And could grab a few hours at the end of the night, rather than the middle. They'd still both be showered and working by the time anyone else arrived in the morning.

Other than Chay, no one else knew that he and Mae were spending their second night at the ISB building. But even if they did, no one would think twice about them doing so. With the case they were all working, they'd probably be more surprised if they weren't.

All of the female agents on the case had been warned to be extra vigilant in the event that Ken Baylor felt trapped, and took his need to conquer the female sex out on those who were interfering with the retirement activities that were feeding him.

Mae spent the first part of their shared "drive" back to Dark Canyon filling him in on the video likenesses Chay and the deputies had been sending her way. She'd positively identified Officer Victor Olsen, whose goose was more thoroughly cooked.

"He was seen a mile from the transition house," she told Jacob. "A week to the day before he was arrested."

Nodding, Jacob tapped the steering wheel, and said, "If the guy's got a brain cell, he's going to start talking and get this done with," he said aloud. "I'll go at him again, tomorrow." The visit to the jail would be one of the first things on his list. If Olsen identified Baylor as even a one-time arm of the trafficking ring, Jacob would have enough to get the sleaze off the streets.

And away from Mae and any other women he might try to target.

She'd made other identifications as well. Two kidnappers who'd been caught and were both dead. And had one possible positive identification on a missing foster woman.

One that had been gone the longest. An early victim. Which could tie Baylor to the ring from the beginning.

There was more. Back and forth between him and Mae. His question prompting her to get up and check a result that led them on to another possibility. It was how they worked. Not every suggestion brought immediate answers, but it led one or the other of them on a tangent that would.

Jacob started to feel better. Stronger. Filled with the determination that drove him every day of his life. Even while, out in the darkness, lingering in his tired brain muscles, and other parts of him, too, was the memory of silk.

"I got through half the blood samples," Mae told him an hour and a half into their "shared" drive home. "So far, there are four matches to fosters whose records were found among those in Baylor's files."

He'd known it was coming. His gut clenched anyway. "Dating how far back?"

"Two years."

He'd known. Had hoped he'd been wrong. "He's had that house for at least twenty. Rented out for ten that we know of for sure…"

"...and that leaves ten unaccounted for." Mae's voice took a noticeable dive, even over the SUV's audio system.

"While I feel certain that he used his political contacts to set this whole thing up, I have to believe that he didn't put the plans into effect until he was out of office," Jacob told her, thinking aloud. "This is a man who puts everything into appearances. He wouldn't risk one of his hoodlums showing up at his office. Or someone trying to blackmail him."

"Not if it meant he could lose his constituency," Mae's words came slowly. "I need to search foster records for the years after he left office and before the records we found."

Silence hung on the line until she said, "Oh my God, Jacob, will this never end? How many women did they get? I keep thinking we're getting to the end of this case, and, instead, for every step closer we take to getting him, we just end up with more possible victims. And he's still out there. Probably making more."

Jacob not only heard the despair in her tone, he felt it in his gut. "We'll get him, Mae. We have to stay strong, focused, and together, we'll get him."

When he heard the words he'd said aloud, Jacob tensed. He shouldn't even have been having such intimate revelations privately, let alone speaking them aloud.

"We do make a good team, don't we?" Mae's voice was too soft. Too...feminine and...like a siren calling out to him in the vast, empty darkness surrounding him.

And he said, "We do."

Knowing that he spoke the truth.

Chapter 10

Lying back against her pillow, Mae stared at the ceiling, at the reflections of lights from her various machines up on the drywall, and talked Jacob the rest of the way home. They talked about the weather. An antelope he saw on the side of the road.

How bitter his coffee was.

And what flavors of creamer they both preferred. She already knew the answers to that one for both of them. Suspected he did, too. But only because they'd been in the same room together pouring their own coffee enough times to notice. They'd never actually discussed the matter before.

They talked about buffalo meat. The cost of eggs. The fact that he needed an oil change. And how long it had been since he'd had his windshield washer fluid filled.

As two hours became two and a half, silence fell. Time in which his mind could drift off. She couldn't let that happen. And said the one thing that was on her mind the second she quit thinking about anything else.

"I've been thinking about trying to find my birth mother. And ask her about my birth father, too."

His answer was immediate. And softly spoken. "Seems like a logical step."

"You'd think so," she told him then. "I think so. And yet, I don't really want to." Which made no sense to her. She was a scientist. Had run her whole family's DNA just to draw a makeup of her own biology. And suddenly, she didn't want to know?

"What's holding you back?"

"I'm not sure," she told him. He was analytical, like her. And was the only one, other than the four people she wasn't ready to communicate with, who even knew she had the issue in front of her.

"Then now's not the time," Jacob said, as though the answer was a given. "You need to know what you hope to achieve before you reach into something so potentially volatile. And be prepared for any eventuality. Or, you at least need to have a strong sense of having to know, one way or another, whatever you might find."

"Yeah." His words made sense. Settled her some. But she asked, "Do you think it's odd that I don't feel any push at all to find out?"

When he didn't answer right away, she started to tense up again. Then he said, "I don't," he told her. "I'm not sure I'd care, if it were me. Someone was in a situation that was wrong for them. They made a choice."

Yep. That's where she'd already been. "She knows I'm out here and has never tried to find me," she added. Then said, "Beyond that, she had to walk away, for whatever reason. Or wanted to. She chose to give birth, but not be a mother. She gave that right, that gift to someone else. She made a different life for herself. I'd have to have a pretty damned good reason for showing up in her world now, thirty years later, disrupting her life. I don't have that reason."

"Give yourself time, Mae. When you know, you'll know."

Such simple words. Filled with the truth. With the myriad feelings swarming around as a result of the shocking discovery, she had no idea how it was all going to play out inside her. And until she knew, she couldn't take action appropriate to her future.

They talked a little more about the situation. Mostly about her parents having kept her birth circumstances a secret from her. The lengths they'd taken to do so. Including pictures of both of them with her at the hospital the day of her birth. Her dad in full-body shots. The ones with her mom just being shots of their two heads together.

She'd looked at them all again as she'd eaten her dinner. And a standout had been how happy her mother had looked.

"You were the answer to their prayers," Jacob's voice came softly over the line.

"Then I was. As I grew up..." And didn't conform to their way of life... She let her words, her thoughts trail off on that one.

"They loved—*love*—you."

Jacob's deep voice came so softly, almost as a caress against the side of her face.

"Yeah," she acknowledged his accurateness. Hadn't doubted that fact, ever. It sat there. A reality that she accepted.

Just as she knew that she loved them.

Jacob rolled into town shortly after that. She waited while he parked. Headed into the building. And then heard, "I'm in my office. Get some rest. We'll talk in a few hours."

"Sleep well," she told him softly. Loath to hang up.

But knowing he was right. They had to sleep or they'd be no good for the case that was driving both of them.

"And, Mae?" She heard the deep tones come over the line as she was pulling the phone away from her ear to disconnect the call.

"Yeah?"

"Thank you."

He clicked off before she could tell him how very much he was welcome.

Which was probably a good thing.

Jacob slept like a rock. And woke on Thursday more rested than he'd been in a while. He spent the morning poring over all of the various pieces of information that everyone on his extended team had sent to him the night before while he'd been gone. Studying. Putting it all together in the way that made the most sense to him.

It was midmorning before he got down to Mae's lab. She was on her stool. Looking at results on her screen. Didn't turn around.

He recognized the dark gray pants she had on as a pair he'd taken out of her closet the day before. Seemed like a week, at least, had passed since then.

"I haven't heard from you all morning," he told the lab-coated back.

She nodded. Moved from screen to screen. Machine to machine. Until he stood beside her. Looking not at the screens that held the information he'd come to find, but at her.

"Mae?"

She turned to look at him, and he saw the darkness in her gaze. The eyes that were dimmed. "I found semen."

He didn't speak. Didn't nod. Just held her gaze for as long as it took.

Seconds passed. She blinked. Swallowed. And said, "Sex trafficking of young women…we suspected," she said.

He nodded.

"I just hoped that the evidence we've found…you know since Fern wasn't…that they weren't, either."

He'd hoped, too. During the odd moments emotions had slipped by his inner control guards. "Fern was held in the cabin on the reservation. Not in the transition house."

The two-bit-thug kidnappers working for Baylor had decided to keep her to sell themselves. They were the ones getting their hands dirty. They wanted some of the big money.

They were both dead for their efforts.

And Jacob had to stay focused on the facts. Let them lead him to the end of it all. "Have you been able to identify whose semen it is?"

Mae shook her head. "So far I only have one sample, and there's no match in the system," she told him. "I did all of the obvious blood samples, first. Just finished them an hour ago. Then started on the rest…"

"How many different blood types?"

"At least fifteen."

He gritted his teeth. Angry that nothing about the case could just be simple. One semen sample that would implicate Ken Baylor. That's all they needed. Or even mucus from a sneeze at the transition house.

Susan had provided them the right to use her son's DNA, garnered from samples taken during his lengthy illness.

They'd collected so much evidence over the past five

months. Had built a solid case in terms of what had been happening right there in the Dark Canyon Wilderness and surrounding cities. Had arrested Victor Olsen, the most ruthless of the dirty cops involved—the one who gave the kidnappers the commands of whom to pick up, and then whom to transport to the border and whom to dispose of when things didn't go as planned.

And still, they had nothing. Because they weren't stopping the degradation.

Yeah, they had Baylor's house. With no way to prove it was his. Or even to put him there. But a man like him, with a well-oiled underground network, would have no trouble finding another hole in which to stash his goods before shipping them out to the buyers he found for them. If Jacob's theory was correct.

He wished to God it wasn't.

Baylor, a smarmy fake who was so good, Jacob couldn't even prove that there *was* a sex-trafficking ring on any kind of a large scale. Fifteen blood types could be from fights going on in the place. So many other samples, from the fighters and from those betting on them. Fern and Annie were kidnappings. And while Jacob and his teams had been able to piece together the fact that Annie's roommate, Camille, had been kidnapped by the same two men who took her—and could find no record of her since—he had no tangible proof that she'd been sold. Killed. Or had escaped and was living somewhere else.

The body at the border, Maura Bennet, fit the trafficking ring theory, but he had no proof that the woman hadn't gone away on her own with someone who then turned violent on her and disposed of her, other than that she was tattooed as Fern had been, and that she had similar chain marks. The chains were common, could be purchased by anyone at any number of hardware stores. Tattoos were an in thing in all walks of life.

And it was all just too much coincidence for his gut to take.

"Have you determined the genders of all fifteen?" DNA from the blood would tell them. It was just a matter of whether or not she'd gotten that far.

Glancing at a screen, typing, Mae said, "I have eleven back so far. All female."

Could be a female fight ring.

Jacob knew it wasn't.

As soon as he had definitive proof of those eleven women being missing persons, he was going to have to contact the FBI. He had to get Baylor first. No way he was going to take a chance that the man had contacts higher up than the Wilson police department.

And the businessmen from whom Baylor had been getting kickbacks? Were they part of something bigger, too? Was it some kind of political pay to play? Or was that simply how Baylor was laundering money to himself?

The questions kept coming. To the point of nearly deafening him.

"We'll find the answers, Jacob." Mae sounded all doctor in that moment. Knowledgeable, confident, and with a calming manner, too.

Meeting her gaze, he remembered his drive back to Dark Canyon the night before. And felt some of his tension slide away.

Mae had known the day was going to be hard. They'd been that way for months. She hadn't expected it to be more grueling in some ways than the hours spent in that transition house hidden away on parkland.

Inside that house, it had seemed as though she could feel the women who'd suffered there, as though she was a part of the horrific crimes inflicted upon them. But at that point, she'd only surmised what might have happened. There was still a bit of hope that they were on a wrong track.

Thursday, in her lab, became a day that would go down in infamy for her. First, from the sheer volume of evidence to test—and then all of the results hitting her so fast she could hardly catalog them all. She had no hope of containing them, one by one, for healthy and manageable mental and emotional processing. She just had to push forward.

At one point, in a state of being overwhelmed to the point of near numbness, she texted Jacob. She wanted her justification for doing so to be because he was the lead on the case, but didn't stop to check whether or not the reasoning rang true. It wasn't like the one piece of information was going to carry more weight than the list of results she had to give him.

But she typed anyway. And sent. Someone who bled in that house was less than two months pregnant. She'd done the quantitative blood test three times. With the same results.

She heard back immediately. Have you run the DNA yet for identification?

Yes. No hits.

Send blood type. I'll start checking with medical facilities, free clinics for young pregnant woman who didn't show for follow-up appointments.

And that's how the day progressed. She produced and Jacob and the teams working with him followed up on every possible lead.

Sassy brought lunch to her. A chicken salad mixture with grapes on a large homemade croissant. She'd brought two trays of them to the ISB building. But hand-delivered Mae's on a paper plate. Along with a homemade chocolate chip cookie.

Mae, involved in cataloging three different sets of results that were presenting at the time, smiled at the woman. Was thankful for her. And took bites, when she could.

Three-quarters of the way through the afternoon, with all of her genetic and hematology analyzers working, she grabbed one of the boxes of evidence she hadn't yet accessed—one that Jacob had labeled as items found in the house, as opposed to possible genetic samples.

She needed a break. A different task upon which to focus. Laying out the items, one by one, checking them against Jacob's list, she verified his work as she went. Until, near the bottom, she picked up a plastic evidence bag and stared.

A toothbrush. Simple, plastic handle, purple. With the bag in hand, she went to her computer and pulled up the entire evidence list that had been created, alphabetically, as a log for the transition house. There was only one toothbrush.

Jacob hadn't said anything about it. Maybe it was nothing. But Mae's heart started to pound as she stared at the item through the plastic encasing it.

The thing was light purple. Which spoke feminine to her. Not necessarily so. Just looked that way to her eyes.

Only one. Were the women forced to bathe, clean up, dress up before they were shipped off? And one toothbrush hadn't been disposed of properly?

Was one of the kidnappers a woman? Was that part of the ruse? A way to lure young women to their captor?

Why would a kidnapper be brushing her teeth at the transition house? Because she'd be staying overnight with the women while they were there. One at a time. There'd only been one chair bolted to the floor.

With exam-glove-covered hands that she had to visibly relax, with deep breaths, to stem their trembling, she pulled the brush out of the protective covering. If she could get a DNA match from that brush, one that was in the system, she might have something to give to Jacob that could end their months-long pursuit. A woman working with Baylor. A partner in crime. Who'd take a deal to roll on the fiend.

Her mind spun ahead of her as she carefully picked up her pair of compound action snips to carefully cut off a small piece of the head of the toothbrush. From there it was quick work to retrieve a DNA sample. And then repeat the process. By the time she was done, the head of the brush was a line of small parts on her table—all labeled—and she had eight samples to run.

The project reignited the fire inside her. Rather than discovering more and more proof of women who'd possibly been sold off, to live or die in purgatory, she had a chance of finding the powers behind the atrocities and stopping them.

If all samples came back the same. And she could identify the woman. Jacob could bring her in for questioning. From there, Mae had no doubt the agent would get the woman to talk. Jacob was that good.

Most particularly with women. He had a magnetism about him that drew them.

Even her. Though mostly Mae was immune to it. Or she had been. Before the whole wedding fiasco. Wanted to be. Would be again.

Maybe. Her mind traveled as she worked, and for once, she let it do so. She needed the respite from evidence of abuse. The lift in spirits thinking of the man brought her. Most particular over the past few days.

Culminating with the night before. She and Jacob had always had a way of knowing what the other was thinking. Which meant they didn't have to talk a lot. So they didn't. Normally. These days they were living weren't normal.

And talking to Jacob had become a thing.

One that she liked.

And maybe wanted to keep. Even when life got back to normal.

Best part was, she was getting the feeling from him that he wanted to continue with their new kind-of-like-a-friendship thing, too.

By the time she had her samples running, other machines had produced results, and Mae continued to move from place to place along her table, keeping careful records of every step she took. Cataloged results. Sent a few to Jacob via text.

Always watching for the toothbrush samples to finish. They'd become her lifeline. A ray of hope in a hopeless world.

And when her phone buzzed a text, she checked that

every time, too. It was her lifeline to Jacob. Though more of the texts were from her parents, mostly her mother, as the day wore on. The woman had started sending her snippets of memories. Things that she held dear to her heart. Moments in time when Mae had shone bright in her life. Mae glanced through them all. Some she was too young to remember. Others she'd forgotten until the reminders came through.

None of which brought any kind of order, or closure to the dichotomy inside her where her identity, or family, were concerned.

One such text, accompanied by a photo, depicted little Mae's excitement in the hospital room when her brother was born.

Biologically. To her parents. She knew her mother's intention. To show Mae that she'd been as important a part of the family, and a happy, well-loved, and wanted child. She had her own memories to give her that. Just wasn't sure how the lies that had been told to her came into play.

She'd just read the text, in its entirety, had glanced briefly at the photo, when a beep told her that the evidence she'd been holding her breath over had produced results.

Hands shaking, she clicked to view them.

Felt her pulse speed up as she copied and pasted, moved to another program, and started a new search. One that could take hours.

Her greatest hope had solidified on the first round. Eight samples, one identity.

If the DNA turned up a name, a person Jacob could

pick up, one who would identify Baylor and anyone else involved, they could finally be done.

As het up as she was, she had to restrain herself from texting him. He was busier than she was, keeping in touch with all of the workforce he was managing, as well as collating, cataloging, and computing all of the different pieces of information they were bringing him. Making certain that protocols were being followed for all of the different agencies involved. And maintaining chains of all evidence that would stand up in court.

He didn't need to hear from her until she had all of the information available pertaining to that toothbrush. He knew she had the implement. He'd documented it. Hadn't mentioned it since.

She could be making a huge deal out of nothing. Letting her emotions interfere with the logic that made her so good at what she did. When she was at the top of her game, her mind could travel intricate lines of science that directed what tests she ran to find things others couldn't.

That was what Jacob needed from her. Her at her scientific best. Not turmoil. Tears. Or even hope.

Dinnertime was approaching when the identity recognition software emitted a soft tone. Looking over from the slide she'd just put on her scope, she saw the confirmation screen. The green letters.

And moved slowly toward them.

Denise Marco.

Typing quickly, she found a whole lot of information. More than she'd wanted.

And texted Jacob.

Chapter 11

With the building clearing out, as most went home for the evening, to get much-needed rest, Jacob had been contemplating a dinner he didn't want—but wanted it to be great enough to tempt his expert forensic scientist to eat—when her text notification sound clicked softly in his too-silent office.

Not waiting to read the long missive after the first words, Got hit on toothbrush, he rushed down to the lab.

As though he'd been looking for an excuse to have a few minutes of quiet Mae time in the lab. Maybe he had. At the moment, he was beyond caring one way or the other about that.

He was far too busy chasing a live and very dangerous demon to worry about intangible possibilities in his personal sphere.

Mae turned as he entered the lab, spinning so rapidly that the hair clipped on top of her head fell forward. She left it skewed, didn't even seem to notice, as she asked, "You know a Denise Marco?"

He shook his head, his gaze steady, focused, as he took in her nuances. Gaining an impression that she was both pleased and disappointed.

"She was a young aide, working for the lieutenant governor's office when Baylor was in office. Her being an aide was why her information was in the system."

Mae turned toward the screens above her table then, clicking a remote, and a photo flashed up on a screen of a woman who could have been a model. Or a contestant in a beauty pageant.

"Blonde, blue eyes, average height, slender—sound like anyone you know?" Her expectant glance hit him square-on.

Jacob scrambled for the second it took him to get in tune with Mae. And then it hit him. "Susan Baylor."

"Right," Mae said, pointing back toward the screen. "A younger version of her. In our dossier on Baylor, it said that he had affairs when he and Susan were married. I think she was one of them, Jacob."

Brow drawing together, Jacob stepped closer to the screen. Studied the woman. "It was her toothbrush in the house?"

"Hers, and only hers, I tested the entire head, piece by piece."

With a nod, he turned to head out the door. "I'll find her," he said.

"No need." The voice behind him no longer held the note of success he'd just heard seconds before.

Turning back, he felt like he physically witnessed the sparkle drain out of Mae's eyes as she said, "She died. Three years ago. Kidney disease."

He swore. Crudely. Not something he did often. Mae didn't flinch. Didn't even seem to notice. Meeting her gaze, he had the sense that she wholly concurred with his assessment.

They didn't speak. Just stood there. Gazes locked.

Until he was getting too much of her for either of their goods and had to break the contact.

Heading toward the door, he went to find them something to eat.

Jacob dropped off a container of shrimp stir-fry an hour after he'd practically hugged her with his gaze over the Denise Marco disappointment.

He didn't look her in the eye, or look at her at all as far as Mae could tell. Just set the container and a glass of tea on the small table where she normally ate, and left.

He'd been on his phone the entire time.

She wanted to believe that the call had been that urgent. But wasn't sure it had been. More like—based on his repeated "uh-huhs"—he'd chosen that moment to check in with one of the many forces he was coordinating in his major effort to stop a kidnapper, trafficker, and murderer.

Hating that she even had the thought, Mae adamantly rejected the idea that her feelings had been hurt by the possible maneuver. And pushed it from her mind.

While she ate, Mae ran and reran identity searches on the blood samples taken from the transition house. Coming up with very little. Which made sense.

If, as they thought, Baylor had been targeting foster women recently aged out of the system because no one would notice they were gone, it made sense that there were no missing person reports popping up.

She'd already received and reconfirmed a couple of hits. One from an arrest for possession of an illegal substance. And the other from an incident involving allegations against a foster father after she'd turned eighteen. She'd given DNA as evidence. From what Mac could find in the court records, the charges had been dropped. Two years before.

The same time frame she was seeing in a lot of the results she was finding. And she texted Jacob. Maybe Baylor came up with the plan to start taking and selling young women after Denise died.

It was just conjecture. But it made a crooked kind of sense, too. He'd needed to fill his house with the illicit female vibe he'd lost. Only he no longer had power, or enough money, to attract someone young enough to fit his ideal.

In her heart, she needed to believe that at least part of the theory was true. Better that the tyranny only traced back two years, rather than the possible decades that the man had owned the remote property.

Turning her complete focus to the items she'd pulled out of the toothbrush box, eager to find anything else that might belong to Baylor or another one of his affairs—a woman who was still alive and could produce the same results that she'd hoped Denise Marco would—Mae stopped at a rope that was different from the others she'd already processed.

Pieces she'd taken herself, from the chair she'd processed at the scene. Other than when she'd pulled it out of the box before dinner, she hadn't seen it before. And hadn't taken a good look at it then, thinking it was just more of the same.

When she actually pulled it out, felt it in exam-glove-covered hands, saw the size of it, her system buzzed with energy. She was holding something different. Longer and thicker than a rope used to tie up slender wrists and ankles.

Not sure what she was dealing with, she tried not to form conjecture. And as she sprayed and swabbed, she wondered if she was looking at some kind of sex toy. The ends were bound, covered with leather handles.

Under her polarized microscope, she was detecting presence of skin. Starting to feel sick at heart again, she reasoned that Baylor could have liked it rough. Not that she wanted to go down that road either, but the idea of someone whacking the guy with the rope she held went down a whole lot better than any other possibility she was trying not to think about.

And then she had to think about them. She had no idea what time it was when she was staring at final results. Late was all she knew.

After analyzing skin samples, she could confirm that at least six of the female owners of blood samples previously tested from the house had been beaten by that rope.

By someone, or ones, wearing gloves. There'd been no male DNA found on the rope. And no fingerprints on the leather-bound ends.

As Mae stood there staring, she was demoralized. For the first time in her life, she wanted to walk away. To leave the lab, quit her job, go and just disappear.

She didn't want to think about tests she could run, ways she could manipulate science to give her a clearer picture, or more definitive proof.

She didn't want to know anymore.

Before she had a chance to text Jacob, who was in his office watching hours of reel from feeds that had come in as far back as anyone had them within a five-mile radius of the transition house, her text sounded.

Grabbing her phone, needing an influx of Jacob more than ever before, she touched her text app, and read,

You didn't come from my egg, my body didn't grow you, but my body nourished you from the first suck. I went through months of hormone therapy and just before you were born, I started pumping so that I would lactate. I fed you for the first time just a couple of hours after you were born. You latched on, and unlike a birth mother, my milk was already in. We'd been told I couldn't get pregnant, Mae. You were my dream come true. And have been every moment since the doctor handed you to me fresh from the womb.

The text covered several screens. Mae moved toward her cot as she swiped. Fell down to it. Read every word.

And just…couldn't anymore.

Couldn't take it in. Bear her mother's pain. Hold her own sense of belonging nowhere. Breathe in one more scent of the chemicals necessary to run and clean her lab. She couldn't carry the weight of the women she hadn't been in time to save. Or accept that there were others out there, perhaps still able to be rescued. And others needing her to prevent horrors from happening to them.

And her mom, suffering to the point of confiding things she'd never voiced, in ways she'd never exposed herself to Mae.

It was all too much.

She was just one average-sized woman who could no longer hold back the tears that had to escape.

* * *

He hadn't heard from Mae. She'd said she'd text him as soon as she had results on the rope. Checking his phone again to make certain he hadn't missed something, Jacob strode from his office. It wasn't like Mae not to do exactly as she said she would.

Or check in to explain the reason for a delay. The woman was 100 percent reliable. Always.

Something he'd come to count on from her. In a way he'd never relied on anyone else. Like a silent promise made between the two of them, they'd always do as they said they would, or check in with an update.

It had been that way for years. At least to Jacob's way of thinking.

Still in uniform, with his gun at his hip, he jogged toward the lab. The doors were locked. The janitor and anyone else in the building overnight had been fully vetted and knew protocol. No one without clearance in or out. No exceptions.

Baylor had found a way to dirty some cops. Had he gotten a ranger as well?

The thought raised Jacob's blood pressure as he burst through the door of the lab. And heard…crying.

Freezing in place, he surveyed every inch of Mae's work area. Looking for something out of place, a clue as to what he might find when he moved slowly forward. If someone was holding her at gunpoint, or…

He didn't get as far as whatever had been on the other side of that preposition. He'd only taken a couple of steps before he saw Mae, long dark hair askew and angling slightly off the center of her bent head.

She looked up. Must have heard him. But didn't try to

hide from him. Not her body, or her anguish. With fresh tears filling her eyes, she looked up at him as though he'd know exactly what was wrong with her.

He didn't. The tears on her face scared him. Unnerved him.

It was the second time that week he'd been witness to them. First, only through sound outside the storage door. He'd been so uneasy then, he'd vacated the premises and hadn't ever let her know he'd been there. Or even bothered to ask her about her distress.

Jacob was at a total loss as to what to do. And, at the same time, as those sharp brown eyes gazed up at him, he filled with purpose. A sense of what he had to do.

Be there.

She watched him as he approached, never taking her gaze off from his. Pulling him to her, or merely holding on, he didn't know.

Didn't matter. Either way, he wasn't leaving.

Sitting down gently beside her, he wrapped his arm around her because it was the only option that presented to him. Just was no other course of action.

And when she leaned against him, he took her weight, naturally, as though he'd done so regularly.

Instead of never.

Her warmth, her softness, even her chemical scent engulfed him in a sense of rightness. Guiding him to bend his head toward hers as he said, "It's okay."

One of the least intelligent things that had come out of his mouth in a while. Clearly, "it," whatever that was, wasn't okay at all.

He couldn't keep his mouth shut, though. "I'm right here," he told her. Not finding the words much better.

Clearly his talents didn't shine in the comforting venue. It wasn't something he'd been called upon to do. At least not since his mother's illness and death.

Yet, as awkward as he felt with his own capabilities, Jacob knew he was absolutely right to be sitting there. Holding Mae.

Absorbing however much he could of whatever had become her last straw.

As her tears quieted, he continued to hold on. There just was no thought not to do so. He couldn't abandon her.

She looked up at him, and his hand lifted to her face without thought. He wiped the tears from her cheeks, staring into her eyes. Telling her with everything he had that she was valued. And more, that she wasn't alone.

That she didn't ever have to be alone. He was always there.

It wasn't an emotional avowal. It was fact. One that he accepted as something that had become a part of him over the years. The idea that he and Mae were a team he could count on.

After accepting his administrations, holding on to his gaze the entire time, Mae reached for her phone. Showed Jacob the most recent text. One from her mother.

He read it. Swallowed. Glanced back at her beautiful face, saw such a lost look in her eyes that he had to wipe it away, at all costs. She wasn't homeless, in any sense.

And her identity was as real and solid as any ever could be. His gaze told her so. And because the situation—all of the situations that had been battering them that week—was so intense, he had to do more than just speak with his eyes.

He had to show her, prove to her just how real she was.

There was no conjecture, no judgment, as he lowered his lips to hers.

There was only instinct.

And need.

Mae's entire universe felt the jolt of Jacob's lips. They were solid. Sure. There. So…there. She tasted his strength, answered his offer, without question. Allowing all thought to fade away. Following him willfully in the oblivion into which he guided her.

She was with him. One hundred percent. That was all that mattered.

When his lips opened over hers, she opened her own mouth, met him tongue for tongue. No hesitation. No question.

Her body flared with need, a secret delicious hunger that engulfed her. She became its willing captive. Ready. Allowing herself to feel everything good that was sheering through her. And to explore the magic of Jacob.

She'd given all she had to good in the world. Was empty of all but the desire to taste and touch the sweet ecstasy that Jacob was offering. He groaned and she grew heady with her own ability to create power between them.

They fell back to the cot together, her hands unbuttoning his shirt, delighting in the opportunity just out of reach. Jacob's chest. Years of looking at it. Looking away from it. Pretending not to know more. To want.

And then her palms were there, spreading over the hair on his chest. Filling with his warmth. Fire spread through her, flames bursting higher and higher as he slid his hands under her shirt, undoing her bra with one quick pinch, his palms covering her breasts.

They didn't rush. Rather, they allowed the pleasure to flourish in one body part and then another, giving time its full glory.

Nor did they hide. As he lay half on top of her, looking down, at the breasts he'd exposed, and then into her eyes, she stared right back at him. Breathing through swollen lips, licking them. A clear invitation.

One he accepted slowly. Watching her as he lowered his head.

The hungry sound that came out of her as his lips finally took hers again was foreign to her. Acclamation and desire all mixing together.

She went for his belt buckle the same time he reached for her pants. His holster was there. Gun still in residence. The blockade didn't slow her down. Didn't still any of the intention inside her. Instead, it ignited her further to take charge of Jacob's most powerful possession. To remove it from his body and lay it carefully down on the floor beneath them.

He pulled down her pants as she was planting the gun, and she turned to see his own also out of the way.

When she saw his nakedness, right there, hard and proud, her heart thudded a celebration she'd never known before. This wasn't just a man, finding mutual pleasure with her. It was Jacob.

The man.

He took a condom out of his wallet, and she helped him slide it on, watching his face, meeting his gaze again, as she did so.

And then, their eyes still peering into one another's,

he slowly slid inside her. Moving gently. Prolonging the suspense, the precious agony.

Until neither of them could hold on any longer.

They went together. Pulsing as one.

And then it was done.

Jacob had no plan for the change to happen one moment to the next. It just did. Within him. And clearly in Mae, too.

As soon as he'd come down, he was sliding out of her. And she was pushing against him. Helping him leave her body in a way that told him it was time to go. Without negating what had happened.

More like it was time to move on.

He did so. Availing himself of her bathroom for the immediacy it offered, giving her time to pull herself together enough to follow behind him, already properly covered, when he exited the small space.

A glance over her table, her screens, gave him a good idea of the last work she'd been doing. Details he had to have. So, he waited for her.

And was ready to process whatever she had for him the second she joined him at her main workstation.

What had been had been.

She was Dr. Mae Copeland. ISB forensic scientist.

He was the lead agent on a case that was going to rock their entire agency. And the state of Utah.

What had happened had happened. It was over.

There was work to be done.

Chapter 12

Mae woke Friday morning sore in places she hadn't been touched in a long time. Lying on her cot in the lab, she stretched, allowing herself a moment to dwell on the memory, and threw back her blanket and prepared for her day.

Fifteen minutes later, she was showered, dressed in black pants, a gray short-sleeved shirt, and at her main workstation, picking up where she'd left off the night before. An hour after Jacob had left. They'd done good work together during the hour he'd been with her after the…incident.

Which had paved the way for her to get the first good rest she'd had in weeks. Maybe months. They'd broken all the rules. But, so Jacob, he'd managed to get them right back on track. The two of them wouldn't speak of it. No one would ever know.

It wasn't like either of them had never had sex before. Just not with each other.

And how great it was to do it with someone who saw it for what it was. Biology. And didn't make a big deal out of it.

Though, it was kind of a big deal, as far as her personal experiences with sex went. Stopping to grab a single-sized bottle of orange juice out of the refrigerator, Mae stood for a second, remembering. And she was flooded with heat all over again.

Jacob Colton was absolutely, hands down, the most incredible lover she'd ever had. And just what she'd needed to rejuvenate her for the long haul in front of her.

The rest—her mother, the work—was normal life. She'd just let it get to her. Had had a bad moment. It happened. Was done.

But the sex... Now that she'd do again. Anytime Jacob was up for it. Smiling at her thought with a silent "no pun intended," she went back to her station. Focused. Determined. And at her best.

Her brain fully engaged.

And emotionally detached. She'd expended a year's worth of the stuff in the half hour she and Jacob had spent together on her cot. Was no longer flooded and spilling over with corticotropin. The fear-inducing hormone. Estrogen had drowned it right out. And was still making her a little warm down below anytime she had a flash of Jacob on her cot.

The man was hot!

And as the morning wore on, Mae was less and less so. She had eleven unnamed female DNA samples on her table. One male, who was not Ken Baylor, or in the system. Most likely one of the hoodlums hired as transport. But not belonging to either one of the two kidnappers they'd had in their morgue.

Using a standard organic extraction method that she'd learned from the justice department, she'd lifted DNA from the fingernail clippings found in the house. It was an arduous process only due to the number of clippings found.

More than sixty of them. Ten fingers, eleven women—assuming some already had short nails, and some clippings were carried out of the house via the bottoms of shoes that stepped on them—she was likely looking at proof that the captive women had their nails cut before they were shipped out. Either for grooming purposes. Or to keep them from scratching their new owners?

She texted Jacob late morning. Nail clippings confirmed matches with seven female DNA samples.

And received an immediate thumbs-up in response.

The purview of their job sucked.

But they were okay. And for that she was thankful.

Jacob was not having a good day. A young woman had been found dead in her apartment in Wilson. Cause of death had been a drug overdose. She'd been a known user, on and off. She'd grown up in the foster system, but had recently been back in touch with a biological brother who'd talked to the police. He thought the girl's death was a murder. Had insisted over and over that she was clean.

That she had everything to live for. They'd been making plans to get a place. He'd aged out of the system a decade before her, had some savings and was going to support her while she went to college.

The reason the police had sent the report to Jacob as an FYI was the new tattoo on the woman's body. Positioned similar to Fern's. And Maura Bennet's, too.

She'd also recently had sex. There wasn't any DNA evidence found on or within her body, but there'd been a little tearing.

There were no ties to Ken Baylor that anyone could find. The woman's records had not been among the fosters found in Baylor's files.

But Jacob knew the girl had been one of Baylor's victims. The man was growing desperate. And more cautious at the same time.

He needed to speak to Mae. And didn't pick up the phone.

The passion that had flared between them the night before was as shocking as it had been unexpected. Had they planned the sex, that would have been different. Not good. But more manageable. He could not condone himself losing control as he had. Without knowing how it had happened, how did he guarantee that it wouldn't happen again?

When all morning long, he'd been buzzing with the desire to do so? To momentarily taste heaven again. To be catapulted out of the horror, the helplessness. Just for a brief respite.

And if he avoided Mae? The job would suffer. Drastically.

The thought had him on his feet, grabbing a photo he'd printed, heading toward the lab with sure steps. The job came first. It always had. What the hell had he been doing all morning, allowing his own self-doubts, his personal lapse to get in the way of the case?

Mae was Mae. Same self-control. Same goals. As they'd proved during the hour of good work the night before. After their interlude on the couch.

She barely glanced in his direction when he walked into the lab, listening to the door swing shut behind him.

"He's changing his MO," he said.

And then she turned, her gaze sharp as it met his. And hung there. Seeking. As always.

"I think he's luring them himself. He doesn't know who to trust, he's used up his arsenal. Or just decided to lay low on the large-scale trafficking since Olsen's arrest, until things quiet down. But he's too twisted to just live quietly while he does so. He hasn't been near the transition house, we know that much, but that doesn't mean he's unaware that we found it."

He set the photo on the table in front of her. Taken by an investigator at the scene. "Her name's Charla Orion. She was found in her apartment in Wilson late yesterday."

Mae's head was bent over the photo for mere seconds, before she turned and looked up at him. "The tattoo."

"That's why the report landed on my desk this morning. FYI only at this point. Official COD is overdose. She's a foster, but not in Baylor's files. Recently had sex, no DNA, but tears."

He laid it all out as he had to do. Didn't even hesitate.

And breathed a little easier when Mae's analytical attention didn't waver. Even for a second.

She'd missed him. Where Mae had always welcomed, preferred, the solitude of her lab over working with the others, the morning had been long and lonely.

Without contact from Jacob. Having him standing there, sharing case details, eased her tension some.

Staring at the photo on her table didn't get any easier. "I'm assuming Wilson police are tracing all of her steps," she started in, focusing. "They've got her cell phone?"

He nodded. She took the motion to pertain to both spoken sentences.

"If they can get me a sample of ink from the tattoo, I can start there. I've got baselines to compare it to. Have them check to see if her nails were recently clipped," she said then. "Check the trash in her apartment for them."

"Already sent that missive. Right after your text."

She nodded. Then said, "I need to see the complete tox screen."

"Check your email."

She did. Saw the message from his account. Opened it. Read thoroughly, but quickly. She knew it all. Recognized what she was looking for immediately. Then turned to look at Jacob. "Check drug suppliers, Jacob. He's getting the gamma-hydroxybutyrate, the same date drug found in Fern and Maura, from someone. Could be her dealer. The amount of fentanyl in her system had been enough to kill a person twice her size. Might be how he found her."

She wanted to stop there. But couldn't. "Unless he's got another source for foster system records." She met his gaze as she laid out the possibility that he had to have already reached.

His jutted chin, and nod, confirmed her supposition. "She was in the system in Page."

Where Melanie Heath had turned up, badly beaten. The woman who was still lying unconscious in the hospital.

Mae swallowed. Focused on the evidence. "What was she doing on this side of the reservation?" Hours away.

"She found her biological brother. He lives in Wilson."

The words hit her deeply. Personally. And she asked, "How'd that go?" If the woman had OD'd…

"Good. He's the one who found her. Called the police."

Her chin tightened. Lifted. But her voice was steady as she asked, "Did he know about her?"

"Yes. They were separated when she was five. He was fifteen. Said he'd been told she was adopted out."

Of note. But not to the job on her table.

"If we're right, and he's digressing, he's more likely to make a mistake," she said then. Something he'd already know.

"And become more dangerous," Jacob said, his gaze pointed as he looked at her. "I want you to carry a gun, Mae. Even down here."

She shook her head. Had fought that battle years ago.

"You're proficient," he told her. "You've passed the tests."

For her job. To allow her to be an active participant in the field where necessary. Not to use it.

She shook her head. "I've agreed to stay here, Jacob. To not go anywhere unaccompanied. I'm not going to carry a gun."

She dealt with the aftermath of death every day. "I'm willing to do this job, to face the darkness every day," she said aloud, meeting his gaze. "I'm not going to point a gun and take a life."

His gaze didn't relent. "Not even if it meant you get yourself killed?" She was already shaking her head when he added, "Or allow someone else to be murdered in front of you?"

She narrowed her eyes. "Give me the damned gun," she told him.

And turned her back.

Mae wasn't happy about the capitulation on a promise she'd made herself years before, and yet, as she heard her lab door close behind Jacob, she was more warm than cold as a result of their conversation.

He needed her safe.

And she needed him alive and well, too.

It was that last that had changed her mind. She would shoot Ken Baylor, or any criminal they came across, if it meant saving Jacob's life.

Law enforcement had eyes on Ken Baylor. The various agencies working together to solve the crimes before them, the dead bodies, Camille's unexplained disappearance in what was known to have been a kidnapper's van, the burned building, the dead kidnappers and jailed police officer—and in Jacob's more immediate circle, the files that had turned up on a warrantless search of Ken Baylor's files—were watching the man as a person of interest.

Jacob just couldn't be sure that they were all watching from the same side. He had complete trust in his agency, the Dark Canyon local police department, and Chay and the Navajo Tribal police. Beyond that, he couldn't afford to believe everything he heard.

Olsen had been a seemingly upstanding member of the Wilson police force. There could be other dirty cops there, too. Likely were, as one man didn't generally pull off crimes to the scale Jacob was suspecting without a small army.

With Ken Baylor having been lieutenant governor,

there was no telling whose pockets he'd lined, meaning anyone walking among them could owe the smarmy man.

Even if they didn't know the extent of Baylor's suspected crimes, they'd remain quiet when questioned about him, speak well of him, to protect their own futures, financial or otherwise.

The scope of what he was facing drove Jacob. He was going to get his man. And it was showing him a side to his own humanity that he'd never met before. He could do all, never give up, put his life on the line, and it might not be enough.

Sassy, who, like the rest of the Coltons, was aware of Susan's negative ties to a potential serial trafficker with murder on his hands, and who was quietly standing with the woman, ready to protect her in any way she could, was making it a point to make certain that those working so hard in the ISB building were eating right. She brought in sub sandwiches and fresh fruit for lunch on Friday. Leaving a disposable foil pan filled with chicken Alfredo in the refrigerator, as well.

"For dinner," she said as she popped her head in Jacob's office door on her way out. "Mae's favorite."

That was it. A few words and she was gone.

Jacob stared after her. Whether his cousin knew that Mae was sleeping in her lab, or that Jacob was spending his nights in the ISB building as well, as added protection, he couldn't say.

But he could guess. Based on the few veiled remarks he'd heard from family members, who'd all managed to get the scientist's name into the conversation, Sassy had laid some ground work. He'd shrugged them all off. Didn't matter whom he had in the lab, the person would play a major role in Jacob's life. As he'd told them all at one time or another.

But as he sat at his desk, with a case that was continuing to pile on, his cousin's not-well-caged innuendo that she knew something was going on between him and Mae didn't bother him as much as it once would have.

She'd had lunch. Alone in her lab. A tuna sub. And while she'd eaten, Mae had texted her mother. The words I love you.

It was all she had to give.

But it freed her attention to more completely focus on the plethora of evidence surrounding her. A couple of boxes that she hadn't even opened yet.

Her machines only worked so fast. And she only had so many of them. Her worktable and the counter along the wall were lined with tests waiting to be run. She'd prioritized based on the evidence lists Jacob had done as he'd logged and boxed up everything that had come in from the transition house.

All morning, with her renewed energy, Mae had been feeling a sense of urgency to figure out what she was missing. What should she be looking for from that house? No one was perfect. There had to be some way to tie Baylor to the place.

Maybe it wouldn't be enough to nail him for human trafficking—yet—but if they could just get him off the street, and behind bars, they could at least prevent further assassinations of young lives.

Reading over the evidence list again, right after lunch, she didn't just scroll through it. She stopped at each item. Contemplated it. And then moved to the next.

Until she found one that stopped her cold. "Wood scrapings." They'd been found on the floor by the chair. Assumed to be a result of multiple victims pulling repeatedly at the chains that had bound them. There were photos of the chair itself, as well as the scrapings where they'd been found, just prior to collection. The chair showed clear damage from the chains.

But the scrapings… Mae stopped… She wasn't sure what about them was catching her. Agents had brought the chair to her. She'd been over it thoroughly before releasing it to the evidence garage. Had already tested all of the samples she'd taken from it.

What more could there be? What might she have missed?

The place hadn't been cleaned in a long time. The scrapings had been mixed in with sediment, dirt, dust. No real way to tell how long they'd been there.

But with no other ideas coming to her, she used tweezers to carefully segregate scrapings and then put the first in her mass spectrometer. What kind of wood? Either matching the floor or the chair. The floor was oak. The chair was beech. She'd already run both of those. From there, something else might speak to her.

In the meantime, she texted the agent in charge of the evidence garage and asked that the chair be returned to her lab.

And then, bringing the crime scene photos of the chair up on her screen, studied them inch by inch. From every angle.

The evidence agent hadn't texted her back. She needed the chair.

Checking to see that all her machines were still engaged, she locked the lab and headed out toward the garage at the back of the building. Stopping, just before she left the building to text Jacob and let him know what she was doing. It was only a few steps outside to the garage. And the sunlight would be good for her. A little serotonin. Just for those few seconds.

I'm on my way.

The text came back within seconds. As she'd half suspected it would. Mae waited, allowing herself to enjoy the few seconds she got to just stand there and watch Jacob walk toward her. Warming at the thought that she knew exactly what was underneath that beige, buttoned-up shirt. Could almost feel the warmth of his skin, the coarseness of the hair on his chest, against her palms.

She almost smiled at him, but caught herself. They were working. Period. The line between the job and anything else was rock solid.

Jacob nodded at her. She bowed her head back.

And they walked silently, side by side, to their destination.

Chapter 13

Standing behind Mae, shielding her, Jacob typed his code to get into the garage. She could have typed hers. He just needed to be in control of the situation.

As a way of maintaining control of himself. He'd been thinking about the woman far too much that day. Worrying about her safety.

Wanting to have another go-round of physical pleasure with her, too.

And Clive wasn't sitting on the bar-height chair behind the counter desk outside the locked evidence room.

"Did Clive know you're coming down to get a look at the chair?" he asked Mae, more uneasy than he'd already been as, hand near his gun, he looked around.

"I called," Mae said. "He didn't answer. I thought he'd run out for a late lunch." She was rounding the counter as she spoke.

"Oh my God! Jacob!"

He glanced her way immediately. In time to see her head disappear from view behind the desk area. Pulling his gun out of the holster, he rounded the structure in one quick spin, ready to take down whoever had Mae.

Then quickly holstered it as he saw the woman bending over his evidence agent.

"He's been shot," she said. "Single to the shoulder. He's lost a lot of blood. Pulse is faint." Grabbing scissors, she cut off a strip of her shirt, tied it around the wound, and then cut another piece and pressed it to the injury itself. Kneeling beside her, Jacob held the swatch in place as Mae stood, pulled out her phone.

Jacob heard Mae speaking to the emergency contact, ordering an ambulance stat, as he knelt beside his fellow agent, his free hand under Clive's good shoulder. Giving the support, the human touch, he dared. Not wanting to do any more damage to his compatriot. "Hold on, Buddy." The words came from him out of nowhere. And just kept coming. "Hold on, we've got you. You're going to be fine."

As he spoke, his gaze took in the scene, cataloging every nuance. Clive had been caught unaware. There'd been no struggle.

And then Jacob glanced up. Saw the frozen image on the screen on Clive's desk. A man in full park ranger uniform. Green pants. Beige shirt. Just like Jacob's.

And wearing the wide-brimmed hat that Jacob put on only when he absolutely had to. The rim of the hat completely blocked the man's face. Other than a white chin covered in dark stubble.

Facial hair similar to Jacob's.

"Get under the desk," he ordered then, in a quiet tone filled with steel as he gently but instantly removed his hand from beneath Clive's good shoulder to pull out his own gun again. Holding it ready to shoot as he kept an eye on the closed door to the evidence room.

He noted, from a corner-of-the-eye view, that Mae immediately followed his directive. Heard sirens coming from the distance, fully aware that anyone inside that evidence room would be hearing them, too.

Jacob cataloged. Prepared.

Heard Mae saying, "Jeanine, trouble in evidence."

Jacob's next-in-command. Jeanine Hall.

"Tell her he's in a park ranger uniform."

He heard Mae's steady words. And knew he'd give his life if that's what it took to protect the woman huddled, unarmed, so close by.

Seconds seemed like hours. They'd been in the garage a couple of minutes and had entered an entirely different lifetime.

Mae huddled, but watched, too. She should be applying pressure to the wound. Freeing Jacob to get into studying the evidence, hunt down who'd shot Clive.

A fellow agent? She couldn't believe that. But an imposter posing as one? Just like the kidnapper who, a couple of months before, had taken Fern while dressed as a local police officer.

Less than thirty seconds after her call to Jeanine, Mae heard sounds outside evidence, the door opening, and then saw agents filing past the desk on both sides.

Jacob stayed with her and Clive. His gun raised, even while he continued to apply pressure to his downed man's wound.

And that's when Mae saw the gun.

"Jacob," she said, softly. "His left arm, the hand is underneath him." She'd noted that right from the start. Was certain Jacob had, too.

"He's holding a gun," she said then. "If he was able to get a shot off…"

She was on the phone again. To local police. Alerting them to a possible injured suspect. Asking for checks at all medical facilities. Putting out a BOLO. As though she was a fully fledged agent, not merely their forensic scientist who'd had field training.

Time seemed to speed up then, with everything happening at once. Calls of "All clear" came from the evidence room, the ambulance arrived, and as Clive was carried off, Mae pulled exam gloves out of the pocket of her lab coat, put them on, and picked up the gun on the floor. Holding it up to Jacob.

"This isn't Park Service issue," she said. "I'll take it to the lab." And headed for the door. Only to find Jeanine right beside her as she reached it.

"Just to be safe," the agent told Mae as she walked the short distance with her to the building and then all the way to Mae's lab.

Neither of them spoke as they made their way through the halls of the building. And while she felt as though she had to excuse Jacob's overkill on his protection of her, Mae was more loath to open the subject of their case lead at all.

Instead, gun in hand, she issued a quick "Thank you" to the agent as she typed in the code at her lab, and went inside to get back to work.

There was no camera footage inside or outside the evidence garage past the still frame Jacob had seen. The cameras had gone offline. Signaling some kind of technical know-how by the perpetrator. Could have been more than one of them. Evidence suggested otherwise.

Not only just the one face onscreen, but the footage

before that of a car entering the lot showed only the driver in the vehicle. They didn't have a license plate, but they had make and model. Jeanine was on all of that.

Right or wrong, Jacob headed straight to Mae's lab when he returned from the hospital. He had pertinent information on the case. Was counting on her to have some as well. Could have called or texted. He needed to see her.

She'd changed her cut-up shirt. Was wearing one a darker gray under her lab coat as she turned, watching as he came fully in the door, walked toward her. He knew because he was watching her, too. Just glad to see her there, safe and well. "Jeanine said the only thing missing from the evidence room was the chair," he said, when their gazes seemed to be saying things that didn't pertain to work.

He still had no idea why Mae had wanted the evidence in the first place. But trusted that her reason was a good one. Which meant the missing chair could be critical. Another lead bullet for him to carry around on his shoulders.

"It was the only piece of evidence in the room pertaining to this case," he said aloud, a fact they both knew. And looked around the lab at the boxes of evidence Mae hadn't released over the months as she didn't know what she might need to compare it with. Thankful that it was right where it was. Chances were, had those boxes been out in the garage, they'd have been missing, too.

"The chair was big," she told him. "Took up space."

He nodded. He'd have been fine with all of the boxes being gone from her space as well. It was normal protocol.

"Every time I looked at it, I saw the women, chained there… I just…"

Jacob nodded again. Stepped up to her workstation beside her as he said, "I know." The words were too soft. Too personal.

He didn't step back from them. But he did change the subject. "Clive's awake," he told her the good news first. "He doesn't remember much, but said he played dead after the guy shot him, and tripped him as he was heading out with the chair. Got his gun. Got a shot off. Thinks he hit him. But heard him pick up the chair and run out. There's no evidence of blood, other than the pool where Clive was lying."

She'd already known that part, he reminded himself. And finished with, "He's going in for surgery tonight. He'll need physical therapy, but the doctors are hopeful he'll regain full use of his shoulder."

Her shoulders let down as tension seemed to drain out of her. Made him want to reach out for them, though. To turn her around and massage the backs of them. And her neck, too.

It had been one hell of a long week.

"He wasn't wearing his gun." Jacob delivered the only other piece of favorable information he'd brought in with him. "Jeanine found it locked in the top drawer of his desk."

She nodded. "I know. She texted," she said. Then looked toward the evidence bag on the far end of her table.

His gaze following her lead, Jacob's gut hardened as he looked at the weapon recovered from Clive's hand, and heard, "It's registered to Victor Olsen."

The dirty cop just kept giving and giving. Even from lock up.

* * *

Mae had other things to tell Jacob. Felt more in control of it all with him standing there, ready to take it on with her.

"The intruder wasn't Baylor." She knocked off the next-easiest-to-prove piece of information. Pulling up a likeness of the body in the video Jacob had seen on Clive's screen, she used her mouse to grab another photo depicting Baylor and laid it over the first. They didn't match up, but that could be due to clothing. Posture. Then, without saying anything, she moved to another screen, manipulated parts of the bodies from copies of the same photos, piece by piece, shoulder to finger, angle of chest, one onto the other, and the discrepancy was too large to miss.

"The disparity in their heights could have been manipulated by boot soles that were covered by the pants legs," she told him. "But not the rest of this."

Jacob stood just behind her, looking at the screens, and when she almost turned around, wanting to raise her fingers to his cheeks, to gently soothe the tension off his face, she stepped aside, quickly, to another keyboard, another screen.

"Clive said he shot his gun, but only one casing, which matched the gun by the way, was found. We assumed that was from the perpetrator shooting Clive. But now I'm thinking the intruder could have been shot, just like Clive thought," she said next, pulling up the computerized version of the morning's events that she'd developed. She didn't pause to see his reaction. Just kept talking. "I drew up the crime scene a little bit ago. Started with the time stamp on the screenshot," she told him, pulling up the program. "Then took everything from there. Based on when we arrived on scene, and the condition in which we found Clive." She clicked and an outline form of the fallen agent appeared on the screen. "We know from the time stamp that no more than twenty minutes passed from the time the assailant arrived, shooting Clive, before we arrived." Intent on her screen, she clicked some more, typed, clicked, and typed, as Jacob leaned in close, his gaze on the screen as an edited version of what took place in the evidence garage played itself out—including Clive tripping his assailant, who'd dropped the chair and then picked it back up—in moving stick figures on her screen. "We only missed him by a few minutes," she was saying, sounding distracted. "Not twenty."

Then kept typing as she listened to Jacob on the phone, giving orders for traffic cameras in the area to be pulled for the more specific times, hoping, she knew, that they'd be able to trace the guy's whereabouts that way. And as soon as he disconnected, said, "Look, Jacob. Based on what Clive said, he'd still been lying where he fell when he tripped the guy. Means the thief had to have come around the desk on this side." She moved her pointer to the right side of the counter.

Before she'd had a chance to say more, Jacob grabbed her hand and said, "Let's go."

The jolt of his fingers holding hers hit her down below, but before she could consciously react, he'd dropped her digits like they were hot potatoes. Another fact she had to ignore for the moment.

"He had to have hit his head," she said, keeping pace right beside him to the door of her lab. No way a human neck could have twisted in the way it would have had to do to avoid the hit. As her program had just demonstrated.

"Just under the countertop covering the desk," he confirmed. Telling her he was already up to speed with what she'd figured out.

"Based on the upward angle of the bullet Clive would have shot, which I was just getting ready to program in, I know basically where to look for that, too," she told him.

And was a tiny bit warmed when he glanced at her with raised brows, glad to have been able to surprise him just a little bit, in the midst of hell.

Armed park rangers were guarding the outside of the evidence garage. They nodded as Jacob escorted Mae inside. He didn't feel good about having Mae out of their secured building with yet another attacker attached to the case on the loose.

One who'd been in possession of a gun registered to Victor Olsen. Guy could be an Olsen underling, left over from when Olsen had still been in action. But someone would have to be paying the guy and it sure wasn't the dirty cop sitting in jail.

Mae found blood under the countertop. Not a lot, but in a spatter pattern. Telling them the thief had likely been grazed by Clive's bullet. From there, based on the line between where they'd found Clive and where the assailant had been for blood spatter, they'd been able to trace a more accurate projection. And found the bullet lodged in a piece of metal framework in the ceiling. As soon as she had the evidence she needed properly bagged and tagged, Jacob escorted her back to her lab.

He wasn't even back in his office before they had a

hit from camera footage. A white truck, single cab, older model that had been seen entering the ISB parking lot just before the time frozen image on Clive's screen, was seen twenty minutes later at a corner one block from the ISB building. The footage wasn't clear enough to get a license plate number, but Jacob asked that detectives send him the footage, and then continue tracking to see if they could tell where the guy went from there.

He'd known the vehicle had to have been on the lot. No way a guy was going to get away while carrying a chair with metal-plated feet around.

What he needed to know was where the guy took the evidence. Or, more accurately, to whom he took it.

In the meantime, he needed Mae to work her magic. Again.

He was in his office only long enough to send the footage that arrived within a minute of his having asked for it to Mae, asking her if she could use skills she'd shown him in the past to enhance the truck's footage to see if she could get a read on the license plate. Which would lead him to the vehicle's owner.

Not that he expected the registration to take him to his perp. The old truck had likely been stolen. Maybe even from an impound lot, since cops were involved.

At least one cop. The perp had shot Clive with Victor Olsen's personal gun. One of them. The cop had turned over his service weapon and a personal one the day he'd been arrested. Swearing that they, in addition to one that had been stolen from him over a year before—a fact he hadn't reported because he felt like a fool for losing it in the first place—were the only ones he'd owned.

A fact that detectives had verified at the time with the license bureau.

Question was, had Olsen lied about the gun being stolen—gasp, what a shock that would be—or had the someone who'd been savvy enough to steal a gun from a crooked cop suddenly decided to use it in a case where Olsen was already implicated?

Jacob knew one man who could answer that question. And grabbed his keys. Victor Olsen might continue to choose not to talk. But Jacob was going to make it as difficult as he legally could to change the crooked cop's mind.

One of his agents had already been hurt. He'd be damned if a second one was going to take a fall.

Chapter 14

There were no windows in her lab. Mae didn't actually see it get dark outside. But she knew by the clock on her cement block wall that it had done so.

She hadn't heard from Jacob, or any other work colleagues, in hours. And while normally she welcomed those days, she was most definitely not living in normal times.

She had a couple of packs of peanut butter sandwich crackers for dinner. With a can of soda. And had done all she could on the evidence garage break-in.

The perp's blood had not netted her an identification on the guy. If she had something to compare it with, she could give a definitive yes or no if it was him. And while she'd been able to enhance the video image of the truck, it hadn't been enough to make out a license plate. Because there hadn't been one.

Nine o'clock was far too early for her to sleep.

And the thought of heading back into wood shavings felt too heavy to contemplate. Young women in trouble were a worse weight to bear, so she went back to the earlier work anyway. Had already had results on the first samples she'd run, before heading to the evidence garage that afternoon.

Several oak, and a couple of beech. The chair had been made from beechwood. Trying to see a pattern, or something that explained to her why those shavings were bothering her, Mae started tests on the next batch of individualized shavings and then pulled up the crime scene photos of the chair again. Filling her screens with all positions.

Ignoring the vibration of her mother's text notification on her phone. Until she just couldn't anymore.

She didn't read the incoming text. Just sent, I'm still here. Need time. Will be in touch. And hit Send. It was the best she could do.

She didn't doubt her mother's love. Or that of the rest of the family. Nor had she suddenly forgotten all of the good memories she had of her childhood. She also wasn't glomming on the many times, from her teens on, when she'd most noticed how awkward she felt around them. How different she was.

That was what had been.

She had to figure out what would be. And to do that, she had to find a way to get in sync with herself.

After hitting Send, she paced the lab. Phone in hand. Wanted to text Jacob, but had no valid reason to do so. She'd let him know about the blood sample producing nothing they could use. The lack of license plate on the white truck. Had it been any other day, any other time, she'd have gone home.

And maybe had she been able to do so, she wouldn't be missing the man who'd been out of touch for longer than usual. Or...being honest with herself...worrying about him.

Jacob had been oozing tension that afternoon. As lead

on the case, he was taking every hit personally. Seeing one of his own agents shot, right there on ISB property, had to have knocked him hard.

Enough so to put himself in danger? Taking risks that could, in a long run, net him the answers he sought, but that would more likely get him killed?

Pacing her lab, she reminded herself that he'd worked jobs every bit as dangerous. That he was the best of the best. Knew how to take care of himself. Even went so far as to reassure herself that he wouldn't dare let anything happen to him until he'd avenged the victimized women and had ensured that everyone responsible for their pain was either dead or paying for the crime.

And when she could stand herself no longer, she gave in and texted him. A private message. You okay?

Telling herself, even as she hit Send, that he wouldn't answer. Because he shouldn't. It wasn't the first time since they'd been on the same team that his life had been in danger. Yet, she'd never sent such a missive to him. The fact that she just had was exactly the reason why personal relationships in the workplace didn't *work*.

They interfered with one's ability to focus 100 percent on doing one's job. All that positivity she'd had that morning, thinking that she and Jacob had pulled off the sex, allowing it to enhance their ability to cope with the difficult stuff and get their jobs done—meaning they could do it again, sometime, when they were both in that place—had just been proved false.

She checked her machines. Looked at other evidence waiting to be tested. Trying to get a feel for importance, to drive her next choice.

And dropped the bag in her hand when Jacob's text

notification sounded. Her first thought was to deny herself the right to look. She was already pulling out her phone before the thought had fully registered.

On my way to you.

On his way to her? To *her*. Her heart flooded, her nerves started to jitter, even as her muscles tightened with tension.

They couldn't do it again. Not two nights in a row. He probably didn't even want to. *She* didn't want to. At least the part of her she could trust didn't.

And then he was there, in her lab. Or rather, in the doorway he was holding open with his foot. As though he wasn't even going to trust her to try to keep her hands to herself. Although, to be fair to herself, he'd been the one to instigate their lovemaking the night before, not her.

He hadn't said a word. Just glanced at her, thoroughly, igniting a spark of hope in her needy body, then reached into the burlap bag he'd been carrying—something she'd barely noticed—and pulled out a holster and pistol.

He held it out. She took it. Had agreed to its presence in her life.

"Put it on," he told her. "From the time you get up in the morning, until you go to bed at night, and even then, it's in reach. Until this case is done."

She studied him for long seconds. Seeing a new tension in him. One she couldn't readily decipher. And she nodded.

"I don't want you leaving the lab without it," he told her as he stood there, watching her strap the smallish 9MM around her waist under her lab coat.

And then, without a word, he walked out.

She wanted to believe the whole thing was overkill. The gun. Him leaving without their usual end-of-shift conversation. But she just didn't. Not anymore.

Jacob grabbed the dinner he'd left reheating, along with a couple of bottles of water, and headed straight back to Mae's lab. She wasn't going anywhere. He had a lot to tell her.

He hadn't eaten since lunch. And even if she'd had dinner, she also had a decent appetite. And if Sassy was right, and the meal his cousin had brought was Mae's favorite, Mae would still munch some.

Back at the lab door in a matter of minutes, with hands full, he tapped against it with his foot, lightly, so she'd know it was him.

And ended up with a gun pointed at his head when the door opened.

"Mae?" he asked, completely perplexed at the hard, determined look in the woman's eyes, and then was even more so when she deflated right before his eyes, nearly losing her grip on the gun as she lowered it.

He saw it slip, saw her catch the thing with her other hand and awkwardly shove it back into her holster.

What the hell! "Are you okay?" he asked, standing there balancing the meal he'd been looking forward to sharing with his compatriot all evening.

There couldn't possibly have been a break-in to the lab, someone there threatening her, in just the few minutes he'd been gone. Could there? About to drop the food and draw his gun, though she'd holstered hers, he saw the drop of her shoulders, the shake of her head, and was already calming the immediate alarm as she said, "The way you're holding that—" she nodded her head toward the food in his hands "—the foil container blocked the peephole."

Feeling like a fool, he strode in as she stepped back. Dropped his load to the table, and turned to her. "I'm sorry," he told her. "I just assumed you'd know I'd be right back." After the night before, there'd been no other choice.

They had to talk, at least.

But beyond that, "We never end a day without…closure of some kind." It was a thing with them.

A texted "I'm heading out," at the very least.

The way she rolled her eyes didn't help his confusion any, but when she walked to the food he'd brought in, lifting the paper plates, plastic utensils, and napkins he'd piled on top, down to the table, laying them out, he relaxed some.

Joined her. About to tell her that Sassy said the chicken Alfredo was her favorite, but stopped himself. Trying to find the line between keeping things professional between them in a friendly way, and just being friends.

The first they'd been doing for years. The second, they couldn't do.

And the sex… Well, that was the most difficult part of the conversation lying ahead. The one he had the most resting on.

But dinner and work, first. To set the stage.

And the rest would follow as it must.

Mae didn't care about society's rules. At least not that night. She was not only relieved, but truly happy that Jacob hadn't deserted her and she wasn't going to pretend otherwise.

Even when it meant telling him that she'd been unable to pull anything useful for him from the garage theft and shooting that afternoon.

Because he pulled back the foil covering what smelled like chicken Alfredo, seemingly needing sustenance as badly as she did, she was willing to wait to have the less-than-stellar report of her activity that was coming. At least until they'd filled their plates.

And had just taken her first bite, when Jacob said, "The shooter's dead."

Mouth dropping open, she sat there, her first bite still on her fork. "How? When?" She hadn't even identified him.

"Tonight. Not long before dark. Still dressed in our uniform. Likely bought it online. Bullet graze on his left ear. He was found dead in the white truck. Just outside of town. Crashed over a guardrail and into a ravine. Likely died on impact."

After chewing the bite she'd put in her mouth, and allowing herself a second to enjoy the taste of her favorite pasta dish, she said, "Well, that was convenient." For Baylor, or whoever was behind the attack, for Olsen probably. And for her, too. Her lack of ID on the guy hadn't hindered Jacob's work.

"A little too convenient," he allowed, accenting the words with his fork. "Tire tracks point to another vehicle coming around the corner in the wrong direction. Forcing him off the road. I've got photos for you to analyze." He took his bite. And as she nodded, added, "In the morning."

"Did you get the chair back?" She might not know why it mattered, but she knew that it did.

"No." The one word said plenty. Mae heard it all. Whoever had killed the thief had taken the chair. Which gave it even more value in Mae's mind.

"Was there signs of anyone down in the ravine, at the scene, post-crash? A trail of tamped-down fauna, if nothing else? Indicating that someone had walked down there and accessed the truck?"

Jacob glanced up at her, a look that made her warm in a good way, and said, "No."

And she knew. "He delivered what he'd been paid to deliver and then got killed for his effort."

Brows rising for a second as he forked another bite, Jacob said, "It looks that way."

"So we're no closer to nailing Baylor. Or anyone else still out there working with him."

"No, but I did get a little something out of Olsen," he told her.

He'd gone to see Victor Olsen again. She should have guessed he would. After his own house had been attacked, his own man hurt… Had she been at her best, she'd have known that's where he'd been. All movement suspended as she watched him. Waiting.

"Stuck to the story that the gun was stolen. Had to be one of two people, according to Olsen. The guy he killed in the hospital the day we arrested him. And the guy who died tonight. The first, Billy, was a thug he let off for brokering drug deals in exchange for work and good money under the table. Not that our friend Victor supplied that last bit of information. He said only that the guy was a known drug dealer and had had a chance to steal the gun once when he'd broken into Olsen's house." Jacob stopped to take a bite. And a sip of water. Then continued. "Olsen claimed that the day in the hospital, he'd gone to get a confession out of Bill. Said Billy had stolen the filled syringe Victor used to kill him and was going to use it on Victor. Insisted that forcing it into Billy's line instead was self-defense."

She nodded. Fork suspended over her plate. Still not eating. She'd heard a version of that part of the tale before. She needed current news.

"Tonight's guy, Shawn McKnight, was the other possibility. He was a deputy working in Oso who Olsen suspected was dirty. Said Shawn used to hang out with him, some. They both liked to hunt. Said he was the only other person in his house during the time frame when the gun went missing."

"He worked for Olsen at some point, but it went sour," Mae translated. "Probably tried to screw Olsen over, get in with the boss, make big money." She watched Jacob shrug.

And went back to eating.

Jacob had more to tell her. But took a couple of seconds to just enjoy sitting across from Mae. And to fully taste his cousin's cooking. It had been a hellish long day.

Not all due to work. He'd never been a have-sex-and-walk-out kind of guy. There were protocols. Kindnesses.

But with Mae, he'd had no other choice but to immediately, succinctly back away from what they'd done. What they had, their work partnership, a whole lot of people were going to suffer if he messed that up.

So thinking, he stopped enjoying just eating with her

and got back to the job. "Olsen was way too confident and seemingly helpful today," Jacob told Mae. The woman's mind worked liked his. And was like a steel trap, too. The way she cataloged and pieced together was invaluable. "Which tells me he thinks he's going to get off. And even get his job back."

Mae's fork stopped midair. She stared at Jacob, mouth slightly open. And, God help him, he wanted to lean over the table and kiss her. Right then and there. "Who else besides his lawyer has he talked to?" In the jail, it all had to be on record. Information Jacob was privy to.

"No one," he told her. He'd already looked there. "Jeanine is checking on his lawyer's contacts, but so far, there's no evidence of him and Baylor knowing each other. But then, if Don James, the lawyer, is a Baylor benefactor, they'd have already found a way to communicate on the down-low."

She nodded. Then said, "There's got to be something with that chair, Jacob. I wish I could tell you why it's sticking with me. Or hit me to begin with. I can't yet. I haven't put it together. But something's there. They risked breaking into ISB to get evidence on the case, not knowing that only the chair was stored out there. Or… Was the chair the only piece of evidence they really wanted and they just got lucky that it was the one piece down there?"

Finished eating, Jacob put his fork down. Held her gaze, tapping into the mental energy that had been alive between them since the first case they'd worked together. "It's possible they took the chair, not knowing it was all they were going to get," he allowed. "Whoever was responsible for cleaning out the truck, then running it off the road, didn't know until they got there that it was all they were going to get..."

She nodded. "I'm assuming you're having the truck brought in."

"Already on its way. It's not going to be easy, getting it out of that ravine." A problem for the tow guys. Not him.

Mae swallowed a last small bite. "It seems pretty clear that Baylor isn't working on his own, even now," she noted, almost casually.

And there he had it. Confirmation of his worst fears. He'd been hoping, since Olsen's arrest, that they'd taken down the key middle portion of the operation.

He had no real way of knowing how many people had been recruited.

But he knew one thing. If he didn't find a way to stop Ken Baylor, get him locked away, evil was just going to keep coming, more lives were going to be destroyed.

And they'd all be lying on Jacob's shoulders.

Chapter 15

"Wait a minute." Mae's mind filled with small icons, mental pictures lining up in a row. She stood and went over to her evidence table. Looking, but not really seeing the sterile boxes with bags inside them.

Then, turned to look at Jacob. "What if, when you went to see Olsen, he already knew McKnight was dead? Or was going to be?" Leaning back against the table, she continued slowly, as thoughts came to her. "Maybe he was the last problem he and Baylor had to deal with."

Jacob stood. Faced her. His gaze locked with hers. "How did they know to break into the evidence garage? Until we found the house, we had precious little of anything that could incriminate them. Other than Olsen's fingerprints on the syringe that was used to spike Billy's IV line. It's bothered me that Olsen wouldn't talk. Wouldn't take a deal to roll on Baylor. Why not?"

She took a step closer to him. "They had a backup plan. A safety valve."

Jacob's chin tight, jutting, he nodded. "A lieutenant governor gets to know a lot of powerful people. Some who he might become aware of having something in a current hidden part of the present, or something in the past…"

"That could be used for blackmail, in the event that one needed a favor."

He took a step closer to her as he said, "A judge who will rule in favor of Olsen's self-defense defense."

"They were planning to stay in business," Mae jumped in. "Olsen knew he'd be exonerated."

Jacob stood still. His gaze on her narrowing. "They know we found the house," he said. "Either Baylor or someone associated went there, saw how we'd left the place, or…"

Shaking her head, Mae interrupted with, "Our people have been watching the place ever since we were there," she reminded. "It has to be that someone with access to law enforcement information, or details from this case, at least, is feeding Baylor information."

"And when they knew we were on to them, McKnight became their fall guy."

Maybe. Mae's mental pictures were finally starting to line up. Energy buzzed through her as she stared at Jacob. "You have to get to that house, Jacob. Now. Tonight."

Drawing back, he frowned at her. Doubt written all over his face. It was a first. His not fully trusting her. Something she'd have to come back to. Didn't matter in the moment. "The chair," she told him.

"It wasn't about the chair, it's about the shavings. The metal plates attached to it. They had to get the chair back so we didn't figure it out."

Spinning, she moved to her workstation. Pulled up pictures of the chair on all screens, just as she'd had them earlier. Felt Jacob's presence next to her before she turned to see him right there.

"Those shavings are by all four metal plates," she told him. Using her mouse to circle each pile.

"They consist of wood from the chair, and the floor."

She glanced at him. Noted his focus on her screens. His nod. And, still watching him, said, "The plates are screwed into the chair and the floor. Every time they're screwed, and unscrewed, they leave shavings." She barely took a breath. Couldn't get the information from her brain to Jacob's quickly enough. The pictures had lined up. "The shavings would be displaced anytime they raised or lowered the floor," she said more slowly. "But it would always end with bolting the chair back down. To be ready for the next victim."

He stared at her then, his gaze intense. Then, with a quick hard kiss to her lips, Jacob headed for the door. "That's where the money is," he said. "In safes under the floor where he keeps his captives."

And he was gone.

Leaving her in total shock.

Jacob had no idea why he'd planted his lips against Mae's as he left the lab. There'd been not one second of thought before it had happened. Nor did he have time to think about having done so.

Already on the phone with night-shift park rangers, he arranged to have one in the ISB building, guarding the hallway outside Mae's lab. If his theory was correct, and the money was under the floorboards—money that Ken Baylor would most definitely have touched—Mae was going to be the one to give them the proof they needed to bring the ex-official to his knees.

And keep him there.

The agent was in place by the time he was heading out of his office, hat on his head, fully loaded gun on his belt, and a knife strapped to his ankle, too.

He wasn't taking any chances.

Rangers who were closer to the transition house than he was were already on their way. And under orders to wait for him before entering the premises unless it had already been breached. If someone was already on the property, or in the house, the armed rangers were under orders to do whatever was necessary to bring down the threat.

While Mae's lab was filled with circumstantial proof of possible wrongdoing, Jacob had no solid proof of crimes having been committed to back up his bold plan. But nothing holding him back from doing so, either. Officially, the home was on parkland. And the owner deceased with no heirs. Even if there'd been beneficiaries, the park could take back the property at any time. They'd just need to compensate the owner for doing so.

On the way-too-long drive for the tension gnawing at him to get to that property, he called Chay, alerting the Navajo officer to his plan. And wasn't surprised to hear that the newly married father had climbed out of bed when the phone rang and would be on the road right behind Jacob.

He called Jeanine, too, just to give her a heads-up, in the event he needed her later that night. In the meantime, she was to get as much rest as she could.

And Mae? He didn't call her.

He'd kissed her. How in the hell did he deal with that?

He couldn't. Not then. Too much was at stake to allow himself to be distracted from what had been a purely knee-jerk, inadvertent thing to do.

He was still forty-five minutes out from the house when his phone started blowing up with calls. Three of them came in almost simultaneously, flashing on the hands-free screen on his dash. Local police just outside the park in the vicinity where the house was located, the county sheriff's office, and his own lead ranger on duty that night. Gut tight, he pushed to hear from his ranger, Bud Ashbury.

"Talk to me," he spit out, his sense of urgency more than clear.

"The place is in flames, man. Sparks shooting so high we can't even get close."

"Don't try," he barked. "Surround the outer perimeter. If whoever set the blaze is still in the vicinity, I'm counting on you to make sure they don't get out."

"Yes, sir," he heard before cutting out.

He took the call from the locals next. Dialing back to hear that the fire department was just arriving on scene of a fire at the transition house on public land.

And the sheriff's office was letting him know that a deputy out on patrol had noticed the blaze and called it in five minutes before.

Frustrated beyond his limit, Jacob jammed his palm against the steering wheel, swore, and rang off.

It had to have been all about the damned chair.

Mae had been right.

And he'd been five minutes too late getting the word out.

* * *

Not knowing what else to do with herself, the second Jacob left her alone, Mae immersed herself in photos of the safe house, homing in on the area surrounding the chair that had been the first thing she'd seen when she'd entered the place.

She was still studying them, memorizing every nuance in case it would help when Jacob returned with whatever evidence he did or did not find, when her phone rang. *Jacob.*

"You haven't had time to get there yet. What's wrong?"

"You up for night duty?" he asked, not quite talking over her, but close.

"Of course. Always. What do you need?"

"You." Her body instantly flooded with a very personal reaction when she first heard the word, the intensity in his voice, but she'd already caught on to other things in his tone when he continued. "The house is in flames. Firefighters are there putting it out. I'm on my way back to get you. We've got leads. No one is taking a twig away from that place, or getting anywhere near it, until you and I have our go at it. Rangers are guarding the perimeter. You and I are going to be standing right there when the fire department issues the safe-to-enter call."

His voice, the tone, was different from any she'd ever heard before. Intense, but in a different way. He'd always been a guy who expected everything of himself, and gave it. But as Mae stood, heading toward her bathroom, and exchanging her lab coat for a sweater on the way, she heard him including her in those highest of expectations.

Something she'd never heard him ask of anyone else. Ever.

It was as though they were one force, not two. The

pressure was on her like never before. And yet, as she hung up from him and finished her preparations to leave, she'd never felt stronger. More sure of herself.

Or ready to get the job done.

Jacob insisted that Mae try to get some sleep on the drive back to the transition house. He was staying on the phone with his ground crew, and with other professional personnel, including the fire departments handling the scene.

And then rested in the car, alongside Mae, when they arrived, and couldn't get close enough to the house to do anything else. His night-shift people were to contact him the second there was anything for him to know. Most particularly if any bodies were recovered, or they noticed breaches of the perimeter.

He wasn't sure about Mae, but he was used to catching sleep when he could, and noticed, the few times he woke up, that her breathing was deep and normal, signifying sleep. At one point, as he lay back in the reclined seat of his SUV, he found himself watching her chest rise and fall with the rhythm of her breaths, noticed the skewed hair clipped as usual on the top of her head, and looked at her face, striking even in slumber, and felt the oddest bit of joy to have her there.

Nothing that made any sense. Most particularly to his half-asleep mind, but there it was. A notice. One he knew he wasn't going to forget.

The memory was his first conscious thought as he awoke, just after dawn, to the sound of his phone ringing, and he raised his seat back up to see smoldering in the distance.

"There's nothing left of the house," Ashbury said, his voice coming over speakerphone so that Mae, who'd woken and returned her seat to its upright position, could hear. "The fire chief will meet you at the end of the drive in with masks and will take you through to get a look. Fire investigators are already on their way so you'll get a full report as soon as one can possibly be done."

Jacob had already started the SUV before the man finished, and was at the drive by the time they got off the phone.

Mae, looking alert and ready, said, "He didn't say if anyone had seen any signs of human remains."

A fact he'd also noticed.

They didn't speak after that, not personally, as the fire chief joined them and they donned respirator masks that made it safe for them to approach the fire site. But made it difficult to converse.

"We've determined where the fire started based on burn patterns," the chief called through his own mask. "No source as of yet. Whoever did this made sure that there wasn't going to be much evidence to allow us to figure out much."

"You're sure it was arson?" Jacob called back. And saw the chief's nod.

The rest of the sight examination was disappointing. No signs of anything but piles of ash.

Mae walked off on her own while Jacob stayed with the chief. Other agents and fire personnel were lingering, looking, trying to find anything that might help them determine how someone had gotten to the house, set a fire, and then disappeared without any of the people watching the structure knowing about it.

He was listening to the chief point out where the flames had been biggest when he'd arrived. The far corner of the house. And telling him that they did everything they could to douse the fire before the entire house was lost, but the beast just kept climbing walls.

"Like he doused the walls, the ceiling, with something flammable before igniting it." He raised his voice to be heard through the mask. And saw the chief nod.

Someone, or ones, had taken a huge chance that they'd get away after ignition. Or they'd dropped the ignition device from a drone. The thought struck, with an immediate note to himself to check airspace, when his phone vibrated against his leg.

His gaze went immediately to Mae, almost as if by rote, and he saw her lift her phone up and wave him over.

He was with her in seconds.

And saw why she'd needed him. She was already taking photos. He did the same. As did others who started to gather around.

With her single-focused scientific mind, she'd gone straight to the area where the chair had been. Scraping through piles of ash with her foot, she'd uncovered a metal plate that had screw holes in it that matched the chairs.

A fireman, after asking if it was okay with Jacob, bent to lift the plate, and they had two of their answers.

The perp, Baylor, Jacob believed, might have come in and out through what looked to be a rudimentarily dug underground tunnel. One that was going to take a ground excavation crew to safely investigate. When he knew where the tunnel led, he'd know where to start checking traffic cameras. He was going to end the crime spree. One way or another.

More incriminating, even than the tunnel, and right beneath the wooden floor where the chair with metal plates had been screwed down to the metal plate covering the opening, stood an open and empty fireproof safe.

Mae had found where the money had been. Explaining why Jacob, with the help of a trained accounting forensic agent in Washington, hadn't been able to trace any money to the man who seemingly had very little of it.

And they still had not one piece of evidence that directly and definitively linked Ken Baylor to the crime.

Chapter 16

Mae didn't want the safe out of her sight for a second. Her determination might not be rational. She didn't care. The thing had to be handled with utmost care so as not to take a chance on a misplaced glove smearing what could be incriminating evidence.

Baylor, or whoever, had to have known that the safe would be found. He'd have wiped it clean. But Mae had ways of getting in crevices that a cloth wouldn't touch, and pulling out one microscopic piece of epithelial that could put a man away for life.

She didn't care how much it cost to get equipment to the site to get the safe lifted properly out of the beginning of the tunnel and into the back of Jacob's SUV. And when Jacob seemed about ready to interject, she quickly said, "I'll pay for it myself."

"I was just going to say that I was already planning to make the call," he told her. Then added, "And ISB will pay whatever expenses are incurred."

She should have known he'd be right on the same page with her. Hated that because of weird-as-hell minutes on her cot with him she was doubting what she knew. About them. About herself.

But then, she was questioning pretty much everything about herself since her biological revelation. And actually welcomed the fact that she was headed back to her lab and was on order to stay there. Sort of. She could leave. But that would require someone else to stop their own lives to follow her in hers, and she wasn't going to take up one more resource minute than she absolutely had to do. They needed every single second of effort spent on stopping whoever was preying on young women.

Being at the house again, it was almost as though she'd felt their spirits, lingering in the ashes. A so-not-her sensation. There was no science to explain the phenomenon and so she tried to let it go.

Jacob interrupted that process when he came in her lab door a while later, wheeling the safe on a cart. And then stood, just looking at her.

"What?" she asked him, her chest tight, breath catching, as she worried that he was about to tell her something she didn't want to hear. Or embark on a conversation she didn't want to have.

Shaking his head, he asked simply, "Are we okay?"

She shrugged. Had nothing left but raw honestly. "If you're asking me how I feel, we're better than okay," she told him, more words bubbling up out of her. "We're under a lot of stress, professionally, and with my recent discovery, I'm drawing strength from us, as a team. We are the one thing I trust right now." She stopped. Heard herself. And quickly added. "Unless that's not good with you. I might be way overstepping my bounds here."

He'd initiated the sex.

And he had kissed her goodbye , too.

But she'd participated willingly, hungrily, in the former, from the start. And hadn't given any sign that she'd been offended by the latter.

"I behaved inappropriately," he said. Was he telling her he had regrets? Trying to let her down easy?

"For people who are purely colleagues, yes, but I invited you to a family wedding, a personal function. You accepted. There's no law against work associates becoming friends. And the rest, as long as both are willing..."

What in the hell was she saying? In trying to let him know he hadn't offended her, she sounded as though she was opening a door further.

He studied her silently. Then nodded, and headed toward the door.

She stood there. Watching him go. Letting him go. Until he was halfway through the opened door. "Jacob?"

Turning back, he stood just inside the lab, the door closing behind him. Sealing in their privacy.

"Are we okay?" She'd given her response. Had a right, a need, to know his.

His gaze holding hers, he said, "We shared an omelet in the car while driving on the way back." As though that it explained it all.

And she guessed, in his world—and hers—it kind of did.

He had at least one man, a killer, on the loose with what he had to assume was a boatload of money. Cash that could be spent anywhere. For anything. Taking in a handful of large bills to purchase a plane ticket might raise an eyebrow. The second he was back in his office, Jacob put in the calls that would get out a warning to all commercial airlines, notifying them to contact authorities in the event a ticket out of the country was purchased with cash.

Someone like Baylor would likely use a private service. And so Jacob got with his Washington contacts and had air traffic control warned to be on the lookout for flights out of Utah and surrounding states leaving the country. Maybe to Mexico, where Baylor could have contacts to whom he sold his goods.

Something had happened to the women in that transition house. And to Maura Bennet, too. Camille had never been found.

He heard from Chay that Melanie Heath, the woman discovered in Page, had regained consciousness but had no memory at all regarding what had happened to her. The woman found dead in the apartment in Oso had died of an overdose that included, among other things, the exact same cocktail that had been used on Fern. Reuniting with her brother, while a good thing, might have brought on some anxiety that prompted a fallback into the drugs that had momentarily softened blows in the past. But that didn't explain the date rape cocktail.

Had Baylor already captured the woman? And then, finding out about her brother, killed her and made it look like a suicide? With the only witness dead, Jacob might never know the answer to that one.

When he was done with the airlines, Jacob moved on to ground transportation. And notices to government agents working border check sites.

From there, he sent out commands for ISB agents, and everyone on his local teams, to check with retailers in the state selling universally accepted credit cards onto which one could load balances. He was reaching.

But wouldn't stop until the job was done. There was just too much at stake.

He also put out notice that until the case was solved, he needed all hands on deck. Agents could take time off for overtime accrued as soon as the case was brought to a close. And heard back from all of them that they'd already committed themselves to being there and helping in any way they could.

He didn't include Mae in the text. She was different.

She'd not only be there, at his request, for her safety, but she'd be working as diligently as he was. There was no time off in their situation. No matter where they were, the case would be driving them. Best put the energy where it would get the greatest results.

And… They were okay. He wasn't going beyond that thought.

His convictions were validated just before noon when she texted him. Success.

She knew he was in the building. He'd let her know, when they'd returned that morning, that unless she heard otherwise, he wasn't leaving her there without him.

Just seemed right, since he worked better knowing where she was, that he give her the same advantage.

With his hair still wet from the quick shower he'd taken, and in a fresh uniform, he headed down to her lab. Noticed first off that she'd changed as well. Into a pair of black pants and gray top he'd seen on her a few days before. Her hair was freshly skewed and maybe even still damp.

He'd had his brother stop by his place to bring him fresh clothes. Mae had the benefit of the stackable laundry unit. One he could borrow.

A flash of memory, silky fabric, hit him for the less

than a second it took him to blink it away. And focus on the screen in front of Mae.

She didn't turn when he came in. Just enlarged the image on the screen.

A partial piece of a bill.

"It's a hundred," she said, talking over her shoulder to him, and then facing the screen again when he was abreast of her. "I was able to enlarge this piece and compared it to all other American bills. And can conclusively tell you that that's the hair on the left side of Benjamin Franklin's head."

The tension in his gut was soothed with a touch of something better, as he studied the screen. She clicked, and showed him the various parts of her process that had led her to the conclusion. One with which he wholeheartedly concurred.

"And here—" she enlarged another portion of the onscreen photo of the thin piece of bill he saw in a hard plastic container on the table in front of her "—is a partial, almost complete, serial number. I can't definitely tell you the year, at least not yet, because I don't have the first letter. I'm going to test inks and other things to see if I can determine the year this was printed. At least it tells us for sure that money was in the safe. In bigger numbers. And if money turns up, this should be enough for a comparison, Jacob…" Her tone was lighter than he'd heard it in a while, filled with a bit of excitement even, and he wrapped an arm around her shoulders, giving her a brief hug, and was out of there.

Mae didn't get anything off the small piece of bill that set it apart from more recent years. Maybe if she'd had the section with the “revolving” bell, made so by color-shifting ink, she’d have been able to narrow it down more.

She did get a bit more from the safe Saturday afternoon. A couple of pieces of thread that she’d picked out of cracks. One on the combination knob outside the safe, used for entry. And the other on the inside top front lip. She used a mirror to see it. And then had her head inside the safe as she pulled it out.

They both appeared to be from the same fabric. She wouldn’t know for sure until she did more testing. I'm guessing a glove, she texted to Jacob. It was the only possibility she could think of that made sense. The inside lip could have been touched by fingers pulling the safe. Or lifting it with the door open. Could also have been left over from some process during manufacturing.

Not so much the front knob. That had likely come from use. And if the strings came from the same type of glove, they’d at least have proof that whoever opened the safe had had his hand inside it.

By itself, the evidence meant little. As did much of the information she spent her days compiling. But as pieces to a puzzle, every single one mattered. They just had to figure out where they fit to know what picture they were putting together.

And until she had more new evidence, she went back to the boxes brought in from the transition house. The wood shavings had been lying in wait for her. And when she’d seen them, she’d known. They’d produced a mother lode. Just not enough of one to nail Ken Baylor yet.

Those boxes represented a lot of busywork. But any one of the items could hold the key. She wouldn’t know until she got through them all. Tedious testing came with the job. And after a night spent sleeping in Jacob's car—something she'd done surprisingly well, finding it…nice…having him there—and then the heightened emotions as she'd handled the safe, she was ready for some ritual testing.

She was eating a leftover sub and chips from the vending machine just down from her lab when her phone buzzed with Jacob's ID on screen.

"Hey," she said as she picked up on the first ring.

"As feared, the tunnel collapsed. Dozers, with agents present, are sifting through the dirt for any potential evidence. Nothing yet. Doesn't look good."

She'd hoped. And knew he had, too. "Where did it lead?" she asked, pointing in the direction that could be the most helpful.

"Dawson Road."

Just that, two words. And a pause. Mae's mind immediately searched for what belonged there and remembered a conversation she and Jacob had had the month before when they first had strong suspicion that Ken Baylor could be involved with the women turning up missing. Because of his former position, investment associations from the past, and being known in the Colton world for his deplorable treatment of his wife, he'd been on their list long before that. But when his records had been hacked and they'd found the list of fosters, several of the Coltons as well as Mae and others had used their various skills to turn up any information they could find on the man.

"Chay found something about that road back when we all did our deep dives," she remembered. "It's a hunting area. Privately owned. Property owners sued for the right to be able to choose not to have cameras allowed in the area." Traffic cameras, overall, were illegal in the state other than where specifically allowed. "Because there'd been an accident at a high-speed curve not far from there, the local police had petitioned to have the cameras set up. The owners claimed that one accident shouldn't change a lifestyle. Part of their complaint had something to do with them being used by illegal hunters poaching off their land. The petitioners appealed to the attorney general for support, and his giving it made a lot of news. From both sides of the spectrum."

"Yep."

"He knew full well that homeowners in the area don't agree with camera use and agreed among themselves, to a point of a community statute, not to use personal ones, either, other than by front doors and only with the scope being directly up by their homes."

"Yeah."

He sounded disappointed. And Mae, who normally just stuck to the things she could prove, said, "So we won't catch him on tape either using the tunnel, or on the road driving away from it. Meaning we aren't going to catch him on the park cameras because he came and went differently. *But*—" she emphasized the word "—we just added another piece of circumstantial evidence to our arsenal. If nothing else, we have more reason to know we're on the right track."

"You busy for dinner?" Mae froze, not sure she'd heard the words right. Not trusting that she'd heard a teasing note in his voice. Jacob wasn't a teaser.

Not knowing what to make of the bizarre question,

since Jacob knew full well she was staying in her lab at his request, she said, "I'm back to the boxes from the transition house." He was the lead on the case. Had a right to know what she was doing.

"I want to bring dinner to you, Mae. Whatever you want. You're always there, working so hard, and the department owes you more than they're ever going to be able to pay."

The department. Not him. He'd made it okay. And yet, the way he'd phrased his initial request made it more. "In that case, I want the casserole my mom used to make all the time when I was growing up. It has ground beef and cream cheese and cottage cheese, green onions, some other things in it."

She had the recipe in her apartment. In the collection her mother had given her as a housewarming gift. Didn't tell him so.

"That's what you want," Jacob's words were more assertion than question.

But she said, "Yes." And hung up.

She was using him to reach out to her mother. Jacob didn't even hesitate as he found the woman's number in Mae's file—an in-case-of-emergency listing—and dialed.

"Hello?" The female voice on the other end was tentative, almost afraid.

Sitting at his desk, Jacob quickly said, "Mrs. Copeland? This is Jacob Colton. I met you last week at..."

"Yes," the woman interrupted. "I know who you are. Is Mae okay?"

Just like her daughter, the woman got right to the

point. Something Jacob respected. And proof that Mae had some of her mother in her, too. "She's fine," he assured warmly. "Working long hours right now as we've got a first-priority case on our hands. She has a request, though."

"For me?"

"The department offered to bring dinner in to her tonight as she's working late and she requested your special casserole. One with cream cheese and cottage cheese and..."

"Sour cream, green onions, yes, it's a pasta dish that she loves. I can have it done in twenty minutes. It bakes at three hundred and fifty degrees for forty-five minutes when they're ready to serve."

"I'll send someone to pick it up," he said, feeling a smile that only slightly reached his lips.

"No, no, don't you worry about that. I know how important you are to what goes on there. I'll send my son in with it."

Jacob hadn't said he'd be coming himself. Only that he'd be sending someone. But she gave him a personal answer. One that told him that Mae talked to her mother about Jacob. In a good way.

"She's still Mae," he said softly. "She just needs a little time to figure that out." And telling the woman goodbye, he hung up.

Chapter 17

Mae had Jacob on her mind the rest of the afternoon. Often just in the background. Finding evidence to end Baylor's reign was front and center. But in those spreads of minutes while she had all of her machines running, had finished preparing the next batch, and was mostly waiting for results, her thoughts went to Jacob, every time.

Ranging from what he'd bring her for dinner after her outrageous and totally unfair ask. To needing to get naked with him again just to show herself that it hadn't been as monumental as she was making it out to be. Emotions were running high.

Doubly so for her, with the whole her-family-not-being-hers-biologically thing. Once the case was solved, and she'd gotten used to being someone different from what she'd thought, she'd look at Jacob and see just the agent she admired again. And the one she most trusted.

Just a normal piece of her life.

Nice, but not earth-shattering.

The way her stomach jittered when he texted just after four to say he was on his way to the lab tried to give lie to the assurance she'd just given herself. But she knew better.

She just needed that one more time on her cot—the experiment that would prove her theory—and she'd be fine.

The second she saw the evidence box in his arms as he came in, she was back to normal. "It's dirt from the tunnel," he told her. "Different sections. I'd like it analyzed so that down the road, when we have access to shoes and boots, we can match samples of dirt with what's on the bottom of them."

She nodded. Then said, "While I'm at it, why don't I sift through it all, just in case I find something we can use?"

He nodded. Said, "Good idea," and was gone.

Saying nothing about dinner. Her mother. Or anything else. He hadn't kissed her. Touched her. Or even stared into her eyes.

He'd set his box on the side counter, and walked out.

Mae was still standing where he'd left her, analyzing the situation, when Jacob was opening the door a second time. Coming in back first, he dragged a hand truck stacked with another five boxes with him.

She watched him stack them all. Was giving him a stare as he glanced her way. And smiled at the closed door as he quietly shut it behind him when he left.

She had a whole night's worth of work in front of her. She had the time. She'd get through it. Was glad to have breaks from looking at blood and other evidence that would prove suffering in the transition house.

While still helping to get them closer to definitively tying the ex–lieutenant governor to the case.

And if Jacob was bringing some kind of really good dinner in—she was leaning toward a choice of filet and baked potato from a local fine-dining restaurant on the next block because she'd had it once at an ISB event held at the restaurant, and she'd raved about it—to compensate her for all the extra work she'd already been doing, then those boxes of dirt were going to earn her something really big.

Like…maybe…one more experiment on her cot, just to set her free.

Jacob was out when the older of Mae's two younger brothers, William, dropped off the casserole. He hadn't planned it that way, but wasn't sorry to have missed any conversation that the man might have had in mind for him, either.

He didn't want her family making more of his relationship with Mae than was there. For her sake. He knew how hard it was to deal with because of what his own family was doing to him. The last thing Mae needed was more familial tension on her plate.

He'd heard that Ken Baylor was at a bar in town, having a drink, and had stopped in, hoping to sit and have a seemingly casual chat with the man. Nothing that would require him to read the man his rights, or have a lawyer present. Just seemingly innocuous leading questions that could give him a read on the guy.

And an opportunity to glean any hint of weaknesses Baylor might be feeling.

Baylor left before he got there. Whether he'd been tipped off—as Jacob had—or not, Jacob had no way of knowing. But he suspected that to be the case.

Jacob had friends and loyal acquaintances all over town.

Ken Baylor, having once been the second-in-command in Utah, and privy to a lot of information the general public never knew, had them all over the state.

He'd just returned and put the casserole in the oven, telling Jeanine that there would be plenty for her and the others, when Mae texted.

Got something.

Setting the timer on the oven in the break room, he went straight to the lab. His gaze seeking out his forensic miracle the second he walked in.

She met his gaze, held it as he came forward, telling him in her own way that she'd found more than just "something."

"I've got your comparable dirt samples," she said first, in the tone that let him know she wasn't at the good stuff yet. Mae had to get to her points in her way. Step by step. "Bring me anything that walked in that tunnel, shoe, boot, bare foot, and I'll be able to tell you what part of the tunnel it was in."

He nodded, his gaze pointing at her intently. "I also found this," she said, turning to her computer and pulling up an image that she greatly enlarged.

"A worm?" he asked when he could tell what he was looking at.

"It's called a nematode and doesn't live on land. This guy was dead when he came in, so he's been out of the water long enough for that to happen. I don't know yet how long that takes, but I will. Most important—" she turned to meet Jacob's gaze "—these tiny worms, tons of them, live in the Salt Lake, Jacob. They need the salty water to survive."

He stared at her. "Whoever was at that house today came from that lake recently enough that the worm was still on his footwear."

She nodded. "I'm guessing it was a pair of lake shoes. It's summer. The lake's filled with mainly only one kind of boater..."

"Sailboats," he said. Remembering trips to the lake with his family when he was a kid.

"And the beaches are filled with swimmers."

Gaze narrowing, he looked at the line of smaller photos along the bottom of her screen. "You find any evidence of white sand?" he asked her. The lake was known for the bright beaches.

She went straight to a series of four photos. Pulled them up.

All four depicted enlarged kernels of white sand. "If I had more time, which I will have, I'll see if I can narrow down an exact beach from what I've got," she told him.

He heard her on his way out the door.

So much for a great dinner. Mae was a little disappointed, but not much as Jacob zoomed out of her lab late that afternoon. She'd not only have done the same, she'd have been disappointed in him if he hadn't. The job always came first.

Most particular the five-month-long search for evidence to stop a man from brutalizing young women. Baylor could be hiding out up on the lake. It was the first actual hit they had that could take them to the man who'd stolen so many lives.

As she stood at her table, going through painstaking attempts to find answers in a plethora of evidence that didn't speak to anything in particular, Mae wondered if maybe the women whose bodies they'd found were the lucky ones. They hadn't had to live through being sold. And then being treated as an object for possibly years on end.

She'd made great progress that day. The safe. The worm. Both strong leads that could get them Baylor at any moment. With any incoming phone call.

And yet, they weren't enough.

If only she could put some of her myriad pieces together. Tie something up that would be enough to at least get some warrants.

They could bring Baylor in. Have legal rights to search his files. His home. His footwear. And his bank accounts.

They knew what had been in them at the time of his divorce. And from what they'd been able to see with some hacking help, they knew he currently wasn't showing near that amount. What they needed to see was if he attempted to move large amounts of cash through any of them in the next few days.

Or opened any new ones.

She'd been through the lists of remaining evidence from the transition house, mind open to anything that jumped out at her. They were listed by room in the house. She had no idea if the women had ever been free to move around the small decrepit place. And determined she'd take the boxes one by one, in the order they were stacked, right after she went to pee.

Sitting in her small bathroom, ready to stand and get back to work, Mae stared at the toilet paper roll she'd just replaced. Everybody had cause to use toilet paper.

Sometimes it ran out and had to be replaced. There'd only been one bathroom in that house.

With a small cupboard under the sink. Which had been right next to the toilet. Made sense extra paper had been stored there. She didn't have any evidence, which told her there hadn't been any there when they'd raided the house. Because Baylor was lying low after the two kidnappers' deaths and Olsen's arrest.

But the little rod that held the toilet paper… It had to be pushed on one end to engage the spring that allowed the other side to fit into the notch that held it.

Mae was up, righted, hands washed, and pulling on exam gloves before she made it back to her table and the box that held everything taken from the bathroom. The cupboard doors. Their handles, which she'd already removed and checked for fingerprints, finding no viable matches.

But she wasn't going to let the strikeouts discourage her. Her career had taught her long ago that, unlike some other jobs, dwelling on what didn't produce only led to failure. There weren't lessons for her to learn from them. Every day was an opportunity to discover something new.

Dinnertime had arrived. She would put together enough snacks and fruit to make a viable meal, but first, she had to get to that toilet paper rod. The agent that had bagged and tagged it hadn't called it that. But there'd been a spool on the list. She pictured a spool of thread. Had guessed it was for stitching up injuries that were too deep for easiest transport to a buyer. And would have been used by someone with gloves on.

The rest of the house had been sterile enough in terms of prints to tell her that much. Probably due to Baylor. Or maybe Shawn McKnight had been sent to do the job. Or, being a deputy, knew to do so. To make sure tracks were covered.

He hadn't bleached the blood, though. Almost as though he'd wanted Baylor to get caught. Could be he'd liked the money, but seeing the women, hearing their suffering had been too much for him. Not all bad guys were rotten to the core.

Would explain why Baylor had had him killed. If he'd known that the man was getting weak on him. More conjecture. Noted in the mental book of what they'd never know for sure.

She'd bet every dime she had that even when they caught Baylor, he wasn't going to shed any light on things for them. Or testify to a damned thing. Like Olsen, he was going to claim innocence all the way. Say he'd been framed. And likely had a judge on the bench someplace in the state who'd rule in his favor.

Which was why they needed concrete evidence that no attorney would be able to refute.

The stuff she was employed to find.

She'd been carefully going through the bathroom box, one item at a time. Open to any possibilities that occurred to her. And there at the bottom was the last item on the list.

The spool. Or, in her vernacular, the toilet paper rod.

Reaching for her dust, and holding the rod in the middle with her free hand, she went straight for ends. Brushed.

And hit pay dirt.

* * *

Jacob was just a couple of yards from Mae's lab door when his phone buzzed her text notification sound. He continued on, giving his short rap on her door, typed in his code, and entered the lab, itching to know what the text was about.

And almost equally caught up in bringing the scientist her wished-for evening repast.

He'd been on the phone since he'd left her lab half an hour before. Coordinating a statewide active search along all routes from Dark Canyon to Salt Lake, which included state police, county deputies, and small-town local police departments, as well as tribal officers, and park rangers on all national parklands.

If Ken Baylor had been the one to take the money and burn down the transition house, and was staying anywhere around the roughly thousand-square-mile lake, he'd be caught by morning. Wanted for questioning only, at that point. Jacob wasn't going to get ahead of himself, and let his eagerness to get Baylor behind bars create any situation that would allow the man's lawyers to get the charges dismissed.

Everything strictly by the book had been his mandate during every one of his phone calls.

The book went out the door as Mae's gaze took in the half-empty casserole dish, the salad, and rolls that had been delivered with it, all lined up on the top of his cart. She froze, then looked up at Jacob and held his gaze.

With some difficulty, he suspected, based on the way she kept blinking, as though fighting back tears. The tremble in her lips gave her away as well. So he did what he had to do. He just proceeded to her small metal table, put out his offerings, including plates, napkins, and silverware from the break room kitchen, then pulled up a stool and dug in.

Because that was them. What they did. They pushed through and got to work. Even when the work included eating what turned out to be an incredibly delicious casserole.

After his first bite, Mae joined him. Almost as though she had to get her share before he ate it all. Which of course, he wouldn't, and based on the amount left, couldn't. She filled her plate. Perched on her stool. Started to eat.

And in between bites, he calmly filled her in on the statewide work he'd put in motion based on her worm discovery. She seemed to be listening, was nodding appropriately as she ate, and so he kept talking.

Giving her more detail in terms of which departments were handling what than she needed. More minute details than he'd ever given her before.

She was eating. Well. Meeting his gaze. And when he finally ran out of roads and byways to specify, she said, "I found a fingerprint."

He set his fork on his nearly empty plate. Wiped his mouth and dropped his napkin on top of his fork. Then, as though he'd just walked in the door for a normal update, asked, "Where?"

"On the toilet paper holder rod," she said, getting up from her empty plate to head over to her screens. She typed, pulled up the rod. Pointed her curser to one end of it.

Mae stared at the screen, not even glancing his way. Her voice was a little off as she told him, "The side a left-handed person would use." With a shrug she added, "Maybe the other side was wiped clean. I just know this is the only place where I got a clear print."

Standing, he joined her at the bigger worktable. Completely focused. Waiting.

She clicked again and a photo came up onscreen. An attractive young woman, looked about twenty to twenty-five, long dark hair, wavy, a little too much makeup, maybe, a butterfly tattoo on her shoulder.

He swallowed thickly. His stomach a little tight on the food he'd just consumed. "Who is she?"

"Her name's Aleisha Stillmore." Mae's voice faded on the last syllable. She turned to look at Jacob then, telling him with her gaze so much more than her words had done.

She was hurting. On overload. But she took a deep breath and, voice gaining strength, told him the rest. "She was arrested for misdemeanor trespassing. She'd been found asleep in the gated backyard playground of a preschool. She was listed as homeless."

Chin clenching tighter, Jacob had to ask. "Is she a foster?"

Turning his way, Mae looked him in the eye as she nodded. And then said, "But she's not on Baylor's list."

And their problem got a whole lot bigger.

Chapter 18

Mae saw the sudden steel take over Jacob's expression and quickly told him, "I think the files Mark's security company hacked were only a small portion of Baylor's files." Then she pulled up copies of the records they had.

"Look at these letters," she said, pointing to the beginning of each foster entry, having studied them so often she knew them by rote. "It just came to me a little bit ago when I was waiting on an ID on the fingerprint."

She glanced over at him, noted his intent attention to her screen, and, gaining back more of her mojo, in spite of the emotional overload, continued to give him her most recent theory. Work was what she did. She was good at it. And happy doing it.

"I thought they were some kind of designation of where the girls were taken. Or what they were sold into. Something about what they were sold for," she clarified. Mostly she hadn't wanted to know those things. They were out of her jurisdiction and were going to hinder her ability to work as speedily as possible.

"It's the same basic twelve letters," she said, explaining her earlier assumption. "But when you correspond them to numbers—it hit me that it was twelve of them.

Twelve letters. Twelve months of the year. What if they're dates? When the girls were taken, or when they were sold. I'm only just guessing here. We don't know that all of these women are missing. We just haven't been able to find current addresses for them. But if they were, and these letters are corresponding dates…look at them."

She clicked to show him the list based on the code she used corresponding the letters with the numbers one through twelve.

Then glanced at Jacob, who looked from her to the list. "Look at the date by Fern's name."

He glanced, was already nodding. "It's the day she was kidnapped."

Energized, feeling a little bit like her old self, Mae continued. "I think this is only the most recent dump he got from whoever, or wherever he's getting it. Which would explain why Maura Bennet wasn't on the list."

His expression grim, Jacob said, "Which means we have no idea how big this thing is."

She nodded. That had already been the case. At least in her mind. "But it also means, once we can legally obtain evidence, and get Baylor in custody, we can get a warrant for this information and definitely tie him to the abductions, if nothing else."

She pointed to Fern's entry. "We've got him dead to rights on this one."

If Mae was right, she'd just proved that there were more women in trouble than they'd known. A godawful thing to take in.

But she survived her job by knowing that her work, the discoveries she made, were what stopped fiends like Ken Baylor cold.

And that's what she had to focus on.

The good her work did for the world.

Not the atrocities she couldn't undo.

For the first time in memory, Jacob didn't know what to do. Standing in Mae's lab, he had no plan presenting itself. No next step. Or thought to what his next move should be. Work always prompted him to action. And in downtime, he had his things he did. Usually with or for his family.

But that Saturday night, standing in Mae's lab, he had nowhere to be except where he was. With Baylor on the loose—and most likely degenerating, based on the empty safe and house fire—the man was going to grow more and more desperate.

Which meant keeping the one person whose science was going to put the man away safe from him. The rangers, officers, and agents out there looking for the man were all in danger as well. Something they knew. Had trained for. And took on willingly every single day when they reported for work.

Mae signed on for science. Not a thief on-site, stealing evidence.

And maybe, just maybe, Jacob had crossed a line where she was concerned. He didn't feel like it. The work was still what came first for him. And for her, too. He had no doubts there. Nor did he find any credence in the idea that he wouldn't drop everything and run, right then, if he had a chance to get Baylor. Or save any life.

Nor would Mae want him to.

But right then, that night, with a nearly sleepless night behind him, no phones ringing, and a state full of agents out looking for their killer, all Jacob wanted to do was be in Mae's presence.

And that was what was wrong. Looking at her standing there, watching him—a look of what appeared inside him as understanding—his duty compelled him to say, "I should be going, getting back to my office, scouring files, searching databases."

She nodded. Didn't say a word to dissuade him. Just kept looking at him.

"I want to sit here with you." He put the problem right out there. They'd spent years solving things together. It was what he knew.

"So sit."

As though to make things easier for him, she dropped down to her stool at the smaller table and started to clear away dinner. Rising only long enough to put the re-covered casserole in the refrigerator. Then reclaiming her seat.

Jacob, who'd been standing exactly where he'd been looking at her screens, watched the whole thing. Unmoving.

She didn't comment. Just sat there. Watching him.

With no other plan presenting, he reclaimed his stool. Folding his hands on the table. Looking over at her. And there they were.

"I think I know what the problem is." Mae's words were a godsend. He latched onto them like a dog to a meat-filled bone. His gaze locked with hers, he waited.

Accepting that understanding was about to arrive. Anytime he was stumped, he came to Mae. She'd been enlightening him for years.

On cases. Always on cases. Only on cases.

They were all he'd ever had questions about. Everything else, he took as it came. Fitting it into his plans for his life, or discarding it.

"It's the sex."

His body reacted to the words in a very not good way. Parts of him that he'd commanded to remain passive jumped to life.

Mae didn't seem to notice. Not even blinking as she held his gaze, she said, "I thought of an experiment earlier that we just need to implement—a test to run, if you will—that should disarm the weapon we unknowingly gave power over us."

Right. Okay. He agreed with disarming the power. Had to acknowledge the power was there in the first place, but with his body parts being attached to him, he couldn't, in that moment, even hope to convince himself he had control over said "power."

"I'm listening," he told her, unable to stop looking into her eyes. The answers were there. He was smart enough to seek them out.

"We do it again," she told him. And his body sent up a second, stronger surge.

Still staring at her—how could he not when she hadn't stopped holding his gaze so intently—he said, "Do it again."

Not a question. Not even an intelligent statement. Just all he had.

Nodding, she said, "The one time, out of the blue like that, with the emotional overload in this lab, the case, my life shock, it was a one-off. Like time out of time. Which is what made it so…unforgettable."

She'd found sex with him unforgettable. His body

liked that, too. A lot. Too much. It was trying to distract his attention from the discussion at hand.

The explanation that would free him to engage in the experiment. The way said experiment would be a solution to the problem.

"All we have to do is do it again, with our eyes open, purposefully. It will be more mundane, and thereby diminish the power the memory of the first time has over us."

The strength of conviction raging through him to give her idea a try concerned him. It came from inside him, as all of his convictions did, but just seemed to be centered lower. With his mind trailing willingly behind.

"Science tells us, hell interviews with pretty much any couple who's been together for a while tell us, that sexual desire diminishes with repetition. In long-term relationships, couples are often counseled to make time for intimate moments or sexual desire can fade permanently."

They weren't in a relationship. Not the kind that had sex as a part of it. For that matter, he'd never been in one. But what she said made sense. A lot of it.

"So do we set a time for the experiment?" he asked her. The idea, as he understood it, was to take away the emotional buildup. The need. "That would make it more clinical," he added in his thoughts.

Lower lip jutting for a second, she said, "I was thinking we just do it. Right now. Otherwise there will be anticipation, which, in itself, is a form of foreplay."

What they were doing right then, sitting there talking about it, was playing with him. A lot.

"There should be rules," he said. Telling himself he

just needed time to think. To make sure that if he engaged in her experiment he wouldn't later regret having done so.

Her gaze was open as she asked, "Such as?"

He shrugged. Drawing a blank. Then said, "Is there kissing?"

Frowning, she studied him for long seconds. Then said, "Yes, I think there should be. Kissing was part of the first encounter and if we leave it out, that aspect remains volatile, unattended."

Right. Like his kissing her goodbye. An involuntary reaction. He saw her logic. Nodded. Then said, "We should leave the lights on. Shining lights on a situation takes away the mystery."

"Okay." Her voice sounded normal, easy, as though she wasn't feeling even a hint of the tension building inside him. "Makes sense since they were on last time, too. We need a repeat, for the act to seem like normal, not something new."

"Right, so you need to go sit on the cot. I'll join you. I'll kiss you." He stopped there. Trying to remember the rest of the sequence. And…couldn't. Memories of sensations flooded his mind. Of Mae. Her essence. Her softness. Her hunger. His body was flaring with a need so compelling it was wiping out thought.

The experiment was designed to rid him of the discomfort permanently. As outlined by the master of figuring out ways to manipulate science to give up all the answers.

He saw her walk over to the cot. Sit down. Knew that the action was deliberately designed, by his own mandate, to call him to her.

And, like some kind of zombie, he stood, approached, and lowered himself to his fate.

Mae remembered need. A sensation so intense it consumed her. Filling her body, her mind so completely that when Jacob's lips came toward hers, she didn't wait for their touch. She reached for it. Hungrily. With a passion that obliterated thought.

His lips, his tongue, were both familiar and brand-new. The recognition ignited something in her she'd never felt before. A sense of belonging in a new dimension. One that was all-consuming. With heights to be climbed, promising ultimate joys. Taking her along a new path that she had no choice but to explore.

Holsters fell away. Guns placed side by side within reach just under the cot. The fully proper and conscientious handling of such giving her a sense of being in control of the experiment. And then Jacob was moaning hungrily as his fingers went for the bottom of her shirt, stripping it off her, and reaching behind her for the clasp on her bra.

Engrossed by warmth, by the tingles his fingers were leaving in a trail on her skin, and by a liquid fire down lower, she fumbled with the buttons on his shirt with trembling fingers. Whimpered as she got to his chest, and then, pushing back against the cot, climbed on top of him.

"It's not the same," he said, as she set her clothed bottom on top of his still-zipped fly. And then leaned so other parts of her were touching him there, while his hands at her hips held her as he pushed up against her.

She heard his words. Met his gaze, and couldn't stop.

"I don't remember exactly what order it went in," she told him breathily.

And then, grinding against him harder, asked, "Do you?" The experiment was important. They had to try to get it right.

"I remember needing to get inside you," he said.

Yeah, she remembered that part, too. They should get at it. So thinking, she sat atop him, scooting enough lower to be able to unbutton his pants. Pull down the zipper. And the elastic on his undershorts.

And then took what sprang free in both hands.

His hands were making quick work of getting her pants down. With her hands all over him, she lifted up on her knees as he slid her fabric down. She wiggled, kicked with one leg, and was free to straddle him. Helped him sheath himself with protection.

Then, looking him straight in the eye, she lowered herself down on him. Sat there. Moved some. Enough to feel him inside her. And then, as though his eyes were directing her movements, she lowered her body down to his, her bare breasts against his chest, and kissed him.

Full on. Tongue to tongue.

His arms came around her, turning her and side by side, they found release. Still looking into each other's eyes.

When it was over, Mae felt the sting of tears.

And pulled away.

Chapter 19

Jacob was no newbie to sex. He'd had his share. Probably more than his share. Enough to know that it definitely wasn't good when the deed made a woman cry.

Could be good in terms of their experiment, however. Or so he told himself as, eyes on her straightening out the pants twisted around one ankle, he grabbed his things and headed to the bathroom.

By the time he was stepping back out into the lab, Mae was at her table. A hand on her mouse, moving it. Then, fingers on the keyboard, she typed. Lifted her right hand back to her mouse and clicked.

A first glance assured him there was no sign of tears. She'd re-secured the hair on top of her head. Tightly. Which struck a note of unease within him.

Most particularly a memory flooded him. Mae's long dark strands running through his fingers. Flowing over his chest.

Lying on the pillow their heads shared as they'd had the most incredible physical experience.

"I just had an idea," she said as though she'd been working for the past half hour. "I should have thought of it when we first got Baylor's hacked files, but I was so set on not exposing that we had them, so I didn't hurt the case, that I focused on using the information we had to catch him."

He was with her on that last part. They had to get the case done. Out of their systems. It was driving them to desperate measures in order to produce enough good feeling and strength within them and between them to keep pressing forward. He'd come up with the theory looking at himself in the mirror in the bathroom.

Had intended to share the explanation with her as soon as he'd reentered her space. But, distracted by her intense attention to the screens, he joined her, taking his usual space just to her right, reading along with her, as she scrolled.

With no idea what he was looking at. Or why. And yet, he was still content to stand there. Taking in the information that seemed important to her. Working on catching up.

"It occurred to me that if we can find how Baylor got access to the foster care records, we could connect the dots that way. If we know who gave him the information, we have another suspect. Or at the very least, a potential witness."

Nodding, he was with her. Still not making a lot of sense of the coding flashing by on her screen.

"So, he might not be working directly with someone in the state's family services department. I've already checked on all the names of current employees. I did that when I got the list, looking for any names that were associated with his. Nothing of note came up. He was lieutenant governor, so there were some crossovers, but nothing that stood out. The state outsources private help in connecting foster families to kids and I'm running a program to see if there's anything on the internet that connects Baylor's email address to any associated with private sector foster family service."

She read. Clicked. Scrolled. And then said, "And if that doesn't work, I can hack into the foster care system and run a check on his email..."

"No." Jacob stopped it there. "You aren't going to risk your career, your good name." He said something he hadn't said to his brother the month before when Mark was using his private bodyguard service to access Baylor's personal files. But then Mark had been hell-bent to protect the nurse he feared the potential traffickers were after. Nothing Jacob would have said would have made a difference.

Mae turned and looked at him then, hardness in her gaze. "Would you risk your own?"

She knew the answer to that one. They had to end the five-month-long case from hell. One that was taking everything from him. From both of them. To the point of using their bodies to find escape, and a sense of pleasure, in order to rejuvenate them enough to go on.

"If you're going to hack, why not just go straight to the state's database?"

She glanced at him, brought up another running program on another screen. And just then the screen stopped. The entire thing was highlighted.

Leaning in, Jacob stared.

He smelled like heaven. A mixture of pure Jacob, the soap in her bathroom, and...her. Mae was looking at the bounty on her screen, but for a second, when Jacob leaned in, all she saw was highlighted lines.

Taking a step back from the screen, she said, "I was wrong."

Frowning, he glanced at her. "Wrong?" He nodded toward the screen. "You just got a hit."

She shook her head. "Not that," she told him. "About the experiment."

His system seemed to slow down, his entire being pulling back, as he stood mostly still facing the screen, but looking at her. A look of remorse on his face. "I'm sorry, Mae," he said then. "I swear to you, I've never made a woman cry before in bed. Whatever it is I did, I'm sorry."

He'd never made a woman cry before. Pleasure hit her on the inside first. Rose to a smile on her lips, as she said, "You haven't?"

His frown deepened considerably. "What's going on?"

"Those weren't upset tears, Jacob. I wasn't crying because I was sad. It was just that...good."

His frown left. So did everything else about him. Completely deadpan, he stared at her, and understanding, she sobered and had to tell him, "The experiment failed."

The side-eyed look he gave her most certainly did not. Fail. She'd shared innumerable glances with Jacob in her lab over the years. Not one of them had lit a fire in her as the one he was currently giving her.

It burned hotter when he said, "Well, maybe we need a detective on the case, along with the scientist." He wasn't teasing.

At least not in a ha-ha kind of way.

"I'm listening," she told him, meeting the problem, and his gaze, head-on.

"It's this case," he told her. "It's gone on too long. We've made headway, but are no closer to stopping the kidnapping. We know it's Baylor, but every chance we have to prove that evaporates before we have our hands on it." As if to emphasize his point, he threw up a hand. It just served to remind her what those fingers had felt like on her body such a short time before.

Thankfully, she was saved from needing to provide a response when he continued. "We're working incredibly long hours, Mae. Neither of us has had a vacation in over a year. We're depleted. And as committed to our jobs as we both are, and being as in sync as we are, we've created a way for us to find some incredible pleasure in the midst of all the pain."

"Go on," she nodded.

"We're seeing the ugliest side of life here in all the evidence, and we're human beings, not robots. It reached a point where, in order to survive, to maintain and continue forward with all of our concentration abilities and energy intact, we had to resort to the most basic of human pleasures. It speaks to our level of trust with each other. That we both reverted, and that we're able to help each other out so well."

"So you think this is just temporary," she summed up, looking for something in his intent blue eyes, not sure what, but finding it anyway.

"I do," he told her.

And she said, "And for my part, add in the whole lost-identity thing, right when we're dealing with so many young women who've had their lives stolen from them." Chin pursed, she was buying into the theory.

Saw Jacob nod. Looking more like himself as he glanced back at the screen.

But she wasn't quite done. "So that means, just until this case is done, if it happens, it does. No big deal."

"Right."

"And we don't have to fight it, if we feel a need to reach out for more?"

He gave her that side-eyed look again. Accompanied by the hint of a grin on his lips. "No," he said. "We don't."

"Then I have to tell you that the highlighted screen you're looking at only means that my system is frozen. The program hit a firewall that it can't get through."

She saw him stiffen. And then relax. Knew he'd caught on, and said, "Maybe, just for tonight, we can turn out the lights, let what happens happen, and then… just fall asleep? I don't know about you, but I could use some good rest."

Jacob didn't smile. He didn't speak. He just walked around the room, turning out the lights.

The sun was already up when Jacob awoke Sunday morning. Lying on his back, on a cot meant for one, he felt the weight of Mae's body half on top of him, her head on his chest, and was tempted to just go back to sleep.

To pretend that the world, and their responsibilities, weren't waiting for them.

She moved against him, probably woken by his change in breathing as he went from relaxed to feeling pushed to get back to work. "It's Sunday," he said. "You feel like some real breakfast?"

Sitting up, Mae grabbed for her shirt, leaving him with cool air hitting his chest as he watched her cover herself. "I'm game for breakfast," she told him. "What are you offering?"

Up and pulling on his briefs, he said, "I'll bring in whatever you want."

She asked for the omelet he knew she'd order. Came with Texas toast from the diner just down from the building. Then, grabbing clothes, she headed into the bathroom without another word.

She'd smiled at him, though. Jacob stood for a second, watching the door, as a wave of warmth spread through him.

Hearing the shower start, he came to his senses and took his leave. A little extra oomph in his step as he headed to his office. Only to be brought fully back to earth as his cell phone rang.

Susan Baylor.

Seeing the battery icon blinking, he hurried to his desk, plugged it in as he answered. So much for personal time with Mae freeing him up to perform his work duties more efficiently.

He hadn't charged his damned phone.

"Jacob? I'm sorry to bother you," his father's girlfriend started in. "But your dad told me I should."

"You can always call me," he assured the woman, pushing by the bit of resistance that came naturally to him as he thought of his father replacing his mother. With his mother's close friend.

And yet, as he stood there, feeling...different—a good different—after the night he'd spent, he was swamped with a new understanding, too. Sam Colton had been devastated when his wife had died. And at sixty-one, the man still had an entire new lifetime ahead of him yet to live. With a woman as kind and dedicated as Susan—not to mention such a great cook—his dad stood to be a whole lot happier.

"Yes, well," Susan was saying slowly, as though still uncomfortable with the call, "I remembered something this morning. Your dad said it's important."

Fully alert then, in spite of the fact that he was in yesterday's clothes that had spent the night on the floor, Jacob said, "Tell me about it."

"Ken kept all of his business private from me, even when we were married. Kept everything in a locked briefcase that he carried to and from work every day. Even kept our joint checkbook in it. And paid all the bills from there."

Jaw clenching, Jacob listened. Susan's words completely gelling with the man he'd grown to know as Ken Baylor over the past months. Prior to that, he'd never liked the man, but hadn't had specific reason not to.

Except that he'd had at least one affair that Jacob had known of, when Susan had been nursing their terminally ill young son.

"I was so busy with Andrew, I was just grateful to have him keeping everything in line for us. He gave me a credit card to use, and paid that bill, too. With Andrew so sick and every test coming back with worse news, I just didn't have the wherewithal to care to see anything for myself."

Jacob pulled out a fresh pair of green pants and a clean beige shirt, piling clean socks and underwear on top of them. Staying busy, which was his way.

"What I remembered this morning was that there was a safe-deposit box. I was missing some jewelry, a necklace, specifically, that I could remember at the time. Ken had given it to me as a gift when I gave birth to Andrew."

Staring at a large mural painted on the long wall of the office, a depiction of a map of the Dark Canyon Wilderness, Jacob was listening intently.

"After our son died, I asked to have the necklace back. Ken kept saying he'd bring it, but made excuses not to. So one day, I went to the bank. Showed my ID. And because my name was on the box, and probably because I was crying, the woman gave me a key to the box. Told me just to keep it. I don't know if that was legal or not, but…"

"Where's the box?" Jacob interrupted.

"Canyon Federal Bank. It's in Oso."

"Do you still have the key?"

"Yes. I just went through my personal lockbox that I always kept in a shoe caddy, and found it."

Instilling as much calm and compassion as he could find in the midst of his urgency, Jacob said, "I'm guessing Ken never knew about the lockbox, or the key?"

"I can't say for sure about the lockbox. He might have found it. But he never knew I had the key and during the time we were married, I kept it in my compact in my purse. One place he'd never think to look for anything."

Already on his way out of the door toward the shower, Jacob arranged to have Susan and his father meet him, once again, on the reservation, where they often had Sunday brunch. And called Chay to find a private room for them to see each other, but not be seen together.

Dropping his stuff on a bench outside the shower, he texted Mae, letting her know he'd be out for a bit and that Jeanine was in the building, and then jumped in the shower.

.All thoughts of sex, and the restful night he'd spent, in the past.

Jeanine brought breakfast in with her and had Mae come into the break room, where sunlight shone in from windows high on the wall, to eat. She provided lunch, as well, in the break room. Saying that Mae needed time outside her lab.

While, in part, Mae knew the agent was right, she also knew that with the specialty lighting in the lab, she was as healthy as anyone with regular exposure to the outdoors would be. And it wasn't like she hadn't just been out the day before. Beyond which, unbeknownst to most of the agents at ISB, Mae spent a lot of Sundays in her lab.

She was never at loose ends there.

And Sunday was the one day a week when she could work without interruption.

In normal times. Which the current ones were not.

She'd barely finished her grilled chicken salad when her phone buzzed a text from Jacob. Smiling at Jeanine, she headed back toward her lab as she read it.

On my way in with mother lode.

Jeanine had said he'd headed out to the reservation to talk with a witness. She hadn't said whom. Mae hadn't asked.

She'd spent the morning running programs and poring over files pertaining to the Utah foster care system. And had information for Jacob, too.

She was just copying and pasting findings into one brief to send to him when he walked in the door of her lab, an evidence box in hand.

"Get ready for a long day," he told her, putting on exam gloves, and reaching into the box to pull out what looked like a bank safe-deposit box.

"I don't think you're supposed to take those," she said, disappointed when she saw what he had. Another collection of evidence that wouldn't stand up in court.

"I had permission from the bank's CEO," he said. "Obtained when the police phoned him."

His heightened tone of voice, as well as the words, gained her attention as she pulled on fresh gloves and joined him at her smaller metal table. Curious to see what he had, she was equally eager to be closer to him for a minute.

Just because it felt good.

He'd said she was in for a long day and, with the case at hand, she knew what that meant.

Grabbing evidence bags and tags, he told her about Susan's phone call, the clandestine meeting on the reservation to get him possession of the key, and his subsequent call to and help from the Oso detective who'd been working with him since Fern Hensley—who was from the small town between Dark Canyon and Wilson—had been found barely alive in a burning shack on the reservation.

"When I saw what was in the box, I didn't want to touch anything," he said, "so we got permission to bring the whole thing back here."

And there "it" was. Enough items to keep her busy for the next week. And based on what she was seeing just lying on top, she was in for the toughest job she'd ever done.

Far worse than everything the transition house had produced put together.

Jacob photographed, bagged, and tagged while Mae started in on making her magic happen. Dark hours were ahead. He knew. Just as he was also certain that they led to the light of day. Literally, he hoped, for some young women.

If he could get to them in time.

"I was able to pull together a pretty comprehensive list of foster women who aged out of the system over the past four years," Mae said as she took the first item, a lock of hair that had been paper-clipped into a curl, to her workstation. "I narrowed them down to those in the southern part of the state, from towns bordering and close to Dark Canyon Wilderness. I might or might not have come across all of the names legally. Some records are sealed."

She wasn't telling him anything he didn't already know. She was letting him know that she'd gone against his dictates and, like his brother Mark, worked outside the law.

"We can't use all the names, but if prints or DNA are in the system, and we get hits, we can verify whether or not they were fosters. I've already identified one. Aleisha Stillmore. The left-handed woman who changed the toilet paper in the transition house. She wasn't on the list from Baylor's hacked files, but she aged out of the foster system two years ago."

Which made her just twenty years old, Jacob translated.

A likely victim. And since her print had been recent enough for Mae to get a clean identification from it, the woman was still probably alive.

Whether or not anyone would ever be able to find her was a possibility Jacob couldn't contemplate. Not while he was bagging and tagging curl after curl from out of a far-too-large metal box.

"We'll find who we find, Jacob." Mae's words broke into thoughts he didn't want to be having, almost as though she was reading his mind.

More possibly, they were of like minds.

"The first priority is to make certain these are the last." He told her what he most needed to hear. To remember.

And he understood something new, too. He and Mae… They weren't just people who shared similar characteristics, or who got along because they were both workaholics. They'd become something new over the past five months.

Something deeper that wasn't ever going to go away.

They were two human beings who'd stayed sane in hell by clinging to each other.

Like marines in warfare, they'd forged a bond that, no matter where they went afterward, would always be with them.

Even if they never saw each other again.

Chapter 20

Mae stayed busy. Focused. The sooner she got through the overwhelming pile building behind her, the closer she'd be to never having to put herself in Ken Baylor's mindset again. Which was what it took to best guess the man's deviousness, therefore, leading her to his probable means and from there to the tests that would nail him.

She suspected the man wouldn't have pulled the locks of hair out of his victims' heads. She wasn't thinking, even for a second, that the man wouldn't have taken pleasure in having done so. To inflict the pain. Because he could. But also to hear the women scream for mercy, making him feel more powerful as the only king who could hand out bits of reprieve. If he felt his subject was deserving of such.

Her assumption was based on the suspected end in mind. Baylor's. Selling the women to the highest bidder. Just as none of the women they knew about had had their faces touched—thus keeping them pretty—the same would be said for the hair. A woman with a bald patch wasn't going to bring as much money.

And since Baylor's bottom line seemed to be power—which he only maintained with enough money to guarantee influence even if it had to be bought—Mae said, "This will be more efficient if I can find matches between these curls and hair samples we've already taken from the transition house. At least that way, I weed out new work from some that's already been done."

She was mostly talking to herself, knowing what the tests involved. But also needing to connect, on a physical level, with the man who was still working from a standing position behind her. Not availing himself of the comfort offered by the stool right next to him.

She wasn't sitting either, but then, she had to move from sample to sample, machine to machine.

When Jacob didn't speak, she continued with her innocuous conversation. Forcing her thoughts onto the train, leveling it before she spiraled and it derailed. "I can compare two samples with the comparison microscope," she said, as though she was teaching a class. "It's the one here, really just two compound light microscopes that are connected by this special piece. It lets me look at two things together, superimposing them into one so that I can detect even the slightest difference between them. Or not."

She'd pulled out all of the bags of hair samples she'd collected and processed from the transition house. There weren't a lot of them. A total of seven.

"I've got twenty-one curls and counting."

Stilling, her hand suspended over a slide, a piece of hair on her gloved hand, Mae nodded. Twenty-one multiplied by the seven samples she had meant a whole lot of comparisons for her eyes to make.

She didn't falter. "For those who don't match the seven for which I've already completed a full analysis, I'll have to look for roots." She prepared a slide as she spoke. Slid it under one of the two microscopes. "Roots are best. They allow me to do a short tandem release analysis. Otherwise, I have to do the longer version. Mitochondrial testing."

"Whatever it takes," Jacob said. "As soon as I finish here, I'll assist wherever I can."

Mae nodded. And got to work with renewed energy.

Stopping for a dinner of leftover casserole when Jacob reminded her they needed to eat.

She was in for a long night.

But she wasn't there alone.

She found six of the seven matches. None of which had DNA registered in the system. And then, with Jacob's assistance, started running samples through her mass spectrometer, to get DNA results for each curl. From there they could run them through databases for possible identification.

Mae looked over the rest of the evidence he'd cataloged in addition to the paper-clipped curls. A couple of necklaces, the cuff of a shirt, a pair of underwear, a bag of rings that Jacob had split up, giving each ring its individual bag. The list went on.

Taking an obvious deep breath, Mae said, "They're trophies."

"And I'm guessing an indication that he liked to meet the women first, before they were shipped off. If we're at all lucky, you'll be able to lift his print off at least one thing here."

He doubted it, though. Baylor had been at it for too

long, getting away with it for too long, to make a rookie mistake like touching items without exam gloves on.

He sat down and did a search in a database open to him of exam glove purchases over the past four years. Came up with a list so long, he saved it and sent it to the inbox of one of the agents on Monday's day shift.

Mae moved from machine to machine beside him as he sat at her computer. As the hour grew later, she didn't seem to slow down, but she had less and less to say, until he couldn't just let it continue any longer.

And there was only one way he could think of to coax her away from the mammoth load of work he'd put upon her.

"It's nearly ten o'clock. Come lie down with me for a while," he said, the invitation coming from his own exhaustion-based longing. "Fully clothed," he amended, as soon as he heard how the words sounded outside his head. "We can set an alarm."

Ready to give her a rundown on how badly they needed sleep, how much more productive she'd be, adding in that her machines could still run while she slept, Jacob was a bit shocked when she looked over at him, nodded, and excused herself to the restroom.

She was back in minutes. "There are spare toothbrushes, in plastic, in a cup in the cabinet," she told him, which was something he already knew as it was standard procedure to keep ISB bathrooms under his watch fully stocked.

As he headed to the room himself, he saw her settle back on the cot, the far side, half leaning against the wall the portable bed was pushed against, and expected her to be asleep when he returned. Was half thinking about heading to his office, to give her more space, when he glanced over and saw her eyes wide open. Watching him.

And knew she'd been waiting for him.

Filing the information away with a bit of good feeling attached, he got himself right to her, and was flat on his back, with her settled against him as though they'd been sleeping that way for years. Instead of once.

She sighed. Lay still. But wasn't sleeping. Her breathing was too filled with thought. He had no other way of describing what he was sensing. Maybe he just knew because he couldn't find a way to let go of all the evidence of horror sharing the room with them.

"When I was a kid, I don't know how old, but it couldn't have been more than four because I was still an only, I used to scare myself with ideas of what the images made by the shadows on the ceiling could be," he said, doing what he could to normalize his mind. "I knew the stories I was making up weren't real. The idea was to find ways to conquer the evils." Even then, he'd been a cop. He just hadn't known it yet.

Her weight had relaxed against him, prompting Jacob to just keep talking. "Sometimes I fell asleep. But other times, the darkness would start to get to me. I'd hear creaks or groans in the house, and head straight for my parents' room." Hard to believe, at thirty-three, he could still remember the sight of the bed. His father on the side by the door.

"I'd walk up to my dad, and just say his name. Really soft. Once. Like it was just between him and me and my mother never knew." He stopped. Felt her hand shift a little on his chest and said, "He'd say, 'Yeah, come on up,' and I'd scurry up and over him, settle in between them. There was never a better feeling than that."

Until right then. Lying on an uncomfortable piece of strung tarp with Mae draped over his right half, her head and one hand on his chest.

It was only temporary. Just as it had been with his folks. Anytime he'd climbed in bed with them, he'd never woken up there. He didn't remember being carried to his own bed, but in the morning, that's where he'd be.

Back then, he'd thought it had been part of that unspoken pact with his dad. So that his mom never knew that her son got scared.

Lying there awake, staring at the ceiling, Jacob thought of the woman he'd adored. The one who'd been the glue that kept the entire family together. The matriarch with all the plans, remembering to include everyone's likes and dislikes into every event.

And then there was Susan. Who, like his mom, thought of others before herself.

After a few minutes of lying there, his right arm wrapped around Mae, he wasn't sure he'd sleep at all. As tired as he was, he couldn't let go of all that was wrong. All that was there. But he didn't move, either. Thinking her asleep, he didn't want to risk robbing her of a second of the rest she so badly needed.

"I remember, too." Her voice came softly in the night. Surprising him. But oddly, not disappointing him. Once again, he and Mae were on the same page. A temporarily, he hoped, sleepless one. Needing the same things.

Easy memories that would take them back to simpler times.

"Before William was born, I used to get worried that

my folks wouldn't want me once the new baby came." Her voice was soft. But fully alert. He'd been thinking she was asleep, and, instead, she'd been lying there thinking right along with him.

He was a bit nonplussed by how glad he was that she was trusting him with her memories. Odd because he'd long accepted that she trusted him completely. On the job.

They were in her lab, in the ISB building, but on that cot, they weren't working. A fact they'd established well in their attempts to de-escalate what had happened between them.

She'd fallen silent. He wanted more. Didn't want to have to ask for it.

"I'd cry sometimes. And some nights, I'd just get up and sneak into their room, lying down on the braided rug on the floor beside my mother's side of the bed. I can remember being about to fall asleep and hearing her covers. She'd call me 'sweet baby' and lift me up into bed with them." She paused. Jacob didn't even want to breathe. Didn't want to interrupt her in the place she'd found. "The baby was there, in her belly. Making it all hard. Taking up room. But when I was there, too, I felt happy."

She'd always been a part of the family. But Jacob fully understood how being in the bed with that unborn baby and their parents made her feel that way.

Instead of lying alone in her own room, feeling like an outcast.

He hugged her. Kissed the top of her head.

And was drifting off when he felt her finally relax into sleep. But as he lay there, he had one last thought for the night. A wish for her.

That someday soon she'd find again the feeling she'd had lying in bed with her dad and her pregnant mom. That she'd allow herself to believe that which couldn't be proved under one of her microscopes. She had a family to which she belonged.

Mae woke up fully alert. Aware of the warm body upon which she lay. She hadn't moved for however long she'd been out. But needed to get up. The evidence on her tables was calling to her.

Moving slowly, carefully, she braced herself against the wall and tiptoed to the bathroom, where she'd left her phone plugged in. Three in the morning. She'd had five hours of real sleep.

After a quick shower, she pulled on gray pants and a black short-sleeved shirt, clipped up her wet hair, and quietly opened the door.

Jacob was at her table, showered, she determined by the damp hair, in fresh clothes, and sipping from a cup of coffee. A second steaming cup sat at her stool.

She glanced at him, caught his gaze, held it for a second, then turned to the caffeine and sipped. Her machines were all showing results. By her second sip of coffee, Mae was recording results. And sending them through the DNA databases.

Then, after putting on more hair samples to run, having to use the longer, no-root approach, she turned to items she'd started brushing for prints the night before.

"What can I do to help?" Jacob asked from his seat on the table where he'd been on his laptop, doing what he did.

"Line up the rings," she told him. "Have them out of

their bags, on top of them, ready for me. We'll do this by assembly line. I'll dust. Those items that provide prints, move to my table. Those that don't can be re-bagged and wait for metal tests. And you could start entering descriptions into the computer and seeing if we get any matches. Maybe we'll get lucky with at least one of them and be able to tell where it was purchased."

It was work she did on a regular basis, on a much smaller scale. If she was lucky, a case might provide one or two pieces of jewelry. Not a tableful.

From one side of the table, Jacob laid out the rings as she'd designated. And on the other, she followed behind him dusting for prints. There were more than she'd expected. Mostly on the outside of the bands from where the wearer would have put the ring on or taken it off.

"My guess is that Baylor wore gloves to handle them," she said, half to herself. "And that he handled them by looping his finger into the ring as the girls handed them out." It was what she'd do. And while Ken Baylor wasn't a scientist, the man had to have had some forensic coaching somewhere along the way.

"The man does seem to have a remarkable ability to be everywhere without leaving a trace of evidence leading to his presence."

"Until now," she told him, looking up to meet his gaze. "We've got him here, Jacob. It's just a matter of pulling it all together."

With a bit of uplift at the corners of his mouth, he nodded. Went back to work.

As did she. The second she found any proof, Jacob would be out the door on his way to put out a warrant for the man's arrest.

She hoped to God all of the law enforcement in the state looking for the man would have located him by then. It was time to end the case.

After months of effort, they deserved to have something come together.

Looking over the table of evidence, Mae knew they'd already been gifted. It was up to her to find the final answer somewhere in the treasure trove the safe-deposit box had turned out to be. And then to expose the bounty.

"It's fitting," she said aloud, her mind traveling a bit as she continued to dust, a basic task that she'd done countless times, "that Susan be the one to expose the fiend."

"And that his mistake came from his first known evil deed of forsaking his own child in his darkest, most painful hours, to go have affairs," Jacob took up. "That's when Susan got a key to their joint box without him knowing she had it."

He'd told her the rest of the story the day before, over dinner.

She'd just found her eighth ring bearing evidence, was opening her mouth to tell Jacob there was a change of plans, she needed to start running the prints she had, just in case one of them was Baylor's, when her mass spectrometer beeped.

As she moved toward it, she turned to tell Jacob, "I've been running some of the hair samples to look for what types of drugs the women had in their systems when the hair was cut."

He got up and came around the table. Joining her by the expensive machine. Was right beside her as she said, "It's a match, Jacob," turning her head to look straight up at him. "The same date rape drug combination Fern,

Maura Bennet, and Annie had in their systems is in this hair sample." She had the hair DNA, if it compared to a sample from one of the fingerprints...

The thought was interrupted when Jacob said, "We have our confirmation that there's one massive movement. And that Ken Baylor, who was the only one other than Sandra permitted to access that safe-deposit box, was involved with all of it."

Holding his gaze, she said, "We just tied him to the transition house."

His eyes lit up with steel and something more as he said, "We just got our proof. At least enough of it to bring him in." Turning, he pulled out his phone just as Mae reached for a fresh slide for the comparison microscope.

His elbow hit her hand, knocking the slide out of her fingers and sending it flying. Downward. Mae moved, but not soon enough.

She stared as the slide embedded in the sockless skin of her ankle, just above her tennis shoe. The glass's intrusion only stung a little.

But the amount of slide missing from view told her she had a bit of a situation.

Jacob was already on the move. "Sit." He led her quickly to her stool. Then, grabbing a paper towel, he quickly pulled the glass and applied immediate pressure to the wound. Reaching for one of her lab towels, he expertly tied that around the wound.

"We've got to get you to urgent care."

There was no room for argument in his tone. Mae had had no intention of giving him one.

Chapter 21

Jacob lifted Mae up off the stool. He didn't ask. He just carried her out.

"I can walk," she said, but her tone sounded more conversational than voicing a complaint and he just kept on walking.

He knew better than to turn quickly in the lab. Most particularly close to Mae's worktable and machines. He'd just gotten so comfortable there over the past week of staying at the ISB building—and sleeping in the space—that he'd failed to follow any protocol at all.

The couple of staff on night duty came out into the hall as he strode toward the back door, and Jacob nodded to the exit. "Cover us, while I get her to my vehicle."

The man, Dennis Mallory, was ahead of him, already pulling his gun and clearing the area. He was at the passenger door of the SUV, his fingers on the handle, when Jacob's fob was close enough and had pulled open the door by the time Jacob was there with Mae.

At a little before four in the morning, the area was not only dark—other than the ISB parking lot, which had been well lit, with full camera coverage, twenty-four hours a day, since the break-in—but deserted as well.

For her part, Mae hadn't said a word. She settled into the seat herself, though. Keeping her ankle elevated with her foot on the dash. Pulling the seat belt to secure herself.

Jacob was worried about blood loss. Mobility loss, depending on what had been damaged by the slash of the slide. "I'm so sorry, Mae," he said as he squealed off the lot and into the deserted street.

"Seriously Jacob, calm down," she told him, sounding almost like an adult chastising a child. "I'm going to need a stitch or two, but I'm fine. And I'm the one who didn't handle the slide as carefully as I know to do."

Didn't matter how she'd handled the slide. She'd have been fine if his big body, his elbow, hadn't plowed into her.

"You need to be on the phone," she told him. "Getting a warrant out for Baylor's arrest."

Pushing the call button on his steering wheel, Jacob phoned Chay, getting the tribal agent out of bed, and told him to get an all points out on Ken Baylor. He was to be brought to ISB holding, and was to be considered armed and dangerous.

Jacob was silent the rest of the drive to the twenty-four-hour emergency care facility closer to ISB than the hospital. He'd screwed up personally, and professionally. A first for him.

And he knew why. He'd crossed boundaries he never should have crossed. Starting with accompanying Mae to the wedding. He'd been dealing with emotional leaks into the business day ever since. He'd have gotten by that, though.

There was only one thing to blame for his less-than-stellar actions on the job.

It was the sex.

Mae was fairly certain no tendons or ligaments had been breached. She couldn't be sure, but from the tiny bit she'd seen before Jacob had wrapped it up, she was fairly certain she was just dealing with a skin wound. Nor was the slice in the area of any major veins.

It was starting to throb. And sting more. Neither of which bothered her beyond the reminder that she couldn't just get back to work.

Taking precious time away from the mountain of critical work awaiting her in the lab was bothering her far more than the cut on her ankle.

Lights were on in the urgent care reception area, but no cars were around, and no one was waiting. For that she was thankful. Hours waiting her turn would be far more excruciating than a cut on her leg.

The woman behind the reception desk stood and greeted them the second Mae, in Jacob's arms, opened the door. Mae didn't want to have to be there.

But she wasn't minding her body being held so closely to Jacob's body. Even with both of their guns in the way.

The woman, in scrubs, eyed the towel wrapped around Mae's left limb, and Mae said, "I just need a stitch or two."

After which Jacob added, "She was pierced by a microscope slide. We don't know how bad it is."

Nodding, the woman opened a door leading farther into the facility. "Let's get you back here on a table and we can do the paperwork from there."

Pulling back a curtain, she showed them into a small

treatment area, then tapped the padded and freshly wrapped table, saying, "Just put her down here. The doctor will be right in."

Mae shivered as cool air hit her where Jacob's warmth had been. And itched to be back at her lab. They'd locked everything up. She wasn't worried about the evidence. She hated that she wasn't there processing it.

"I hope this doesn't take long," she told Jacob, who was pacing the small space. His gaze mainly on her ankle. "I want as much evidence as I can provide when Baylor is brought in. Enough to hold him. No way I can even think about that guy getting out on bail."

Jacob's phone rang then, and Mae watched him intently as he answered. Hoping that from her lips to God's ears, Ken Baylor had just been picked up.

"Yeah," Jacob said, turning his back on Mae. And then, "Right." Followed shortly by "Let me know." Before the lead agent hung up. And turned.

"There've been no hits on Baylor anywhere near Salt Lake. Officers and agents spent the night going into every bar, every restaurant, then every twenty-four establishment, every motel, hotel, and gas station and didn't get reports of even a single sighting of him."

Mae took a deep breath. Let it out in a loud sigh. "It's like we're chasing a ghost," she told Jacob, but turned as the curtain moved and the doctor, a man about her age, came in.

At which point, she braced herself to endure whatever had to come.

Mae had been right. He should have known. While there'd been a lot of bleeding, she'd only needed two stitches. There'd been no damage to ligaments or muscles. She had a bandage covering the recently stitched skin, and was free to walk out of her own accord.

Before the sun had even started to rise. She was more frustrated about time lost in the lab, and no word regarding an arrest.

"It's got to end today," she told Jacob as he turned the SUV back toward the ISB building.

He was with her on that.

The two of them had become such an item in his life he wasn't even sure who he was some of the time. Like the night before when he'd held her and felt compelled to offer her comfort.

It wasn't a bad thing, if not done at work. And by someone else.

It just wasn't him. Or Mae, either.

The Baylor case, carrying on for so long, the hideous crimes, was all taking its toll. They just weren't themselves.

But they were getting the job done. "You tied Baylor to the transition house," he told her then. "That's the break we've been looking for."

She might have nodded. He didn't look over again. Was on a plan to try to not connect with Dr. Mae Copeland, other than to discuss tests, experiments, and findings.

At least until he had a chance to get his head on straight.

Without traffic, lights were all in his favor, staying green, and he was just a couple of minutes away from the ISB building, where he'd see Mae to her lab and then excuse himself, when Jacob's phone made a sound he had heard before. And a message popped up on his dash screen.

"It's a notice from the alarm system on your dad's house." Mae said aloud what Jacob had just read. Leaving her to decipher the rest, he floored the gas.

"No one answered the phone," Mae said. "Police are on the way."

He sped through the streets, every nerve in his system jabbing at him. Susan. The safe-deposit box. Even if the woman hadn't been behind the find, Baylor would suspect that she'd be the one responsible for the theft of his souvenirs.

"The bank doesn't open for several hours yet. How would he know that anyone accessed the box on a Sunday?"

Cocking his head, his jaw tight, Jacob said, "Same way he's known every damn thing else. He's still got someone on the inside. Keeping him one step ahead us." He had to get there in time. He'd kill the man with his bare hands if he'd hurt his father or Susan.

"He's a coward," he said aloud. "He goes after defenseless women. And hires tougher men to do the dirty work for him." He had to remind himself of the fact.

And mentally compel his father and Susan to hold on. Sam would know that help was only minutes away.

Jacob's heart sank a little further when he noticed that he and Mae were first to arrive at his father's home.

Squealing around the corner, he took note, and said, "Keep the doors locked and stay low. The police should be arriving any second." And had barely stopped the car before he tore off.

Her foot still numb from the shot the doctor had injected in the wound before he'd stitched her, Mae had no intention of just sitting. Jacob couldn't possibly predict what he was getting into. And with no one else there, he'd have no hope if Baylor was waiting inside for him.

With a trap set.

She wasn't an agent. Had no intention of pretending differently. But she was acutely observant. Knew how to hide. And how to shoot the gun Jacob had insisted she wear.

She'd never ever imagined herself pulling the trigger of anything aimed at another human being, but if the beast, Ken Baylor, was hurting anyone else, she'd do it. Without hesitation.

Shrugging out of her lab coat, she opened the car door quietly and slid out, keeping low just as Jacob had told her to do. Praying that cop cars wheeled up before she'd taken too many more steps.

Learning all kinds of new things about herself, Mae kept hidden in the darkness by the shadows of the bushes lining the side of the property. It was sometime between five and six. She should have looked.

The sun would be rising a little after six. She had to have a plan for that.

Jacob had a key to his dad's house. Mae had watched him enter through the front door. Listened for gunshots. Hearing none, she wasn't sure if that was a good thing or bad. Had Baylor been lying in wait? Knocked out Jacob?

Did the man have Jacob's gun?

Keeping low, she made a run from her bush hideaway, across the grass, to another set of shrubbery around the side of the house. Stopping, she crouched. Listened. Then moved slowly toward the corner of the house. She'd round to the front, inch her way to the window, and get a look inside.

The police would be there by then. She could tell them what she saw. If Jacob was tied up, being held hostage, she could give the arriving officers the information they'd need to rescue him.

She wouldn't let herself think about Sam and Susan. Hoped to God they'd made an impromptu choice to head to the popular southern Utah vacation mecca of St. George after having told Jacob about the safe-deposit box.

But knew the thought was more civilian than scientist. Had Sam been safely ensconced in a luxury hotel, he'd have answered his phone.

She was almost there. At the corner of the house. One step. Just one more.

Then…slam! She took a blow to the back of her neck.

And went down.

As soon as he was in the house, Jacob knew something was wrong. He'd seen the broken glass on the floor by the back door.

He'd called out, had no response, and tore through the residence, starting in the kitchen, looking for…god knew what. He prayed not blood.

Finding nothing downstairs, turning the lights on in the darkness as he ran through rooms, he'd torn up stairs he'd climbed a million times growing up, heading to his parents' bedroom, with a lump in his throat and hatred in his trigger finger. Gun raised, he flattened himself against the wall, and then, with a quick spin, planted his feet in the room, gun aimed. And hand on the light switch. Immediately bathing the darkened room in light.

Highlighting Susan. She started to sob the second she saw him. Tied up, with a gag in her mouth, she kept cocking her head to her right, with tears streaming down her face. With his eyes on her, he approached, his gun ready, but needing to reassure the loyal blonde chef as well.

He was only a foot from Susan when he saw what she'd needed him to find. His father. Sprawled on the floor, unconscious.

Heart pounding, Jacob knelt down, felt his dad's pulse. Was reassured at least by the strong, steady rhythm, and then dialed for an ambulance.

Hanging up immediately to ungag Susan.

"Where is he?" he asked as the gag fell from her lips.

"I don't know," the traumatized woman whispered. "He came in, knocked your dad out before he was even fully awake. Hauled me out of bed, tied me up, and said the police weren't coming. Said he has real friends, someone on the Dark Canyon force, and the alarm was canceled."

Jacob had the woman's hands and feet free, and grabbed his phone. Quickly dialed Chay. Told the man to call Jeanine and anyone else he trusted and get an army out to his dad's house.

Then, kneeling in front of Susan, he took her trembling hands and asked, "Where is he now?"

"I don't know." The woman still whispered, as though she believed her evil ex-husband was still close. "He heard your car, or saw the lights or something, and ran out."

Jacob was already at the bedroom door, heading to the hall, when she finished the sentence.

The back of Mae's left shoulder and neck ached. Pain shot into her head and down her back when she moved that arm. But her thoughts were as clear as the sight that was showing the gun pointed just off to the left side of her head. Baylor had forced her back inside the house.

To die with the rest of them, she was pretty sure.

She had no intention of doing so. She had to be alive to process the evidence of what the man had done. She had his prints on her clothes.

And some of his skin under her fingernails. They had him. Completely. Totally. No doubts.

Finally.

"Walk," the man hissed in her ear, just as steps could be heard from upstairs.

"Don't move." The words called out so close to her ear, Mae heard ringing after they were done. "You move and I shoot her."

Ken Baylor yanked Mae in front of him with a hand on the back of her neck, using her as a shield. The barrel of his gun pressed hard against the skin behind her left ear. Just above the bruising that was going to be a whole lot more serious than the two stitches in her ankle.

She couldn't move, couldn't risk being shot for doing so. And couldn't see who Ken was talking to.

"Back up," Ken ordered, while pushing her forward at the same time. Toward a staircase.

He was going to take her life and leave her with the rest of them. Reality hit like a result on her spectrometer. Just there. And yet…leaving cause for error as well.

Machines were generally infallible. Human beings never were. No matter how prepared they might be, there was always the emotional cortex that could turn traitor. She had to play on Baylor's emotions somehow. Get some kind of power over him.

And not think about whoever was upstairs, having attempted to escape, and being forced to head back into the hell that would end in death.

If she could stall long enough, the police would get there. If Baylor was still in the residence, and she was still alive, he'd use her again to get himself free.

And the one agent Mae would be able to count on to get her out of that fire would have been Jacob Colton.

Picturing him lying on a floor upstairs, she prayed that he was still alive.

Thankful that the man didn't know about the less-than-an-hour-old stitches in her ankle, she forced herself to keep her steps steady, in spite of the sting every time she bent her ankle.

Jacob? Was he still alive? Susan? Sam? Who'd managed to survive? She had to know in order to be able to calculate.

Baylor's hand dropped from her neck to grip her hair. She bit back a cry as he twisted his fingers under her clip that had fallen to the back part of her head, forcing her chin down to her chest as he pulled her hair into a tight grip. Raising his gun arm and pressing the weapon's muzzle more deeply into her skull, he said, "Get back in there or I kill her."

"Step up," he hissed to her, yanking straight toward the ceiling on the hair he held. Shoving her chin so fiercely into her chest that she could taste blood in her mouth.

Mae had never been filled with such bile-inducing hate. But she stepped. Until something else occurred to her, she had to follow orders. To do whatever it took to keep herself alive.

"Stand in the doorway," Baylor called out then. "Stay where I can see you or she dies." And yanked up on Mae again. Then again. Each step, another hard yank. Not because he had to do so to get her to comply.

Jacob, she cried silently. *Hang on. We'll figure it out. We always figure it out. And... I'm so glad we had the sex. If I die... I'm glad to have shared that with you.* The words kept coming, filling her mind as she climbed, distracting her from the pain Baylor was inflicting.

It was getting light outside. The sun was rising. She prayed that it shined on them as Baylor yanked her hair yet again.

The psycho took pleasure in causing pain. How Ken Baylor had ever been elected to the second-highest position in the state, she had no idea.

At the top of the staircase, Baylor stopped. Keeping her head forced downward. His body so close behind her she could feel him pressing up against her. And nearly threw up.

"Let her go, Baylor. Take me." At first, Mae thought she was hearing the words in her head, dreaming them up from the conversation she'd just been having with Jacob.

Jacob. He was there. Alive. He'd been able to step back into the room. And to talk.

He'd spoken for her sake. It hit her. He'd known there was no chance in hell of Baylor letting her go. Jacob would shoot him dead. Her lead agent had just let her know that he was there. Still fighting. She had to fight. He was counting on her to do her job.

Just as he was doing his. It was what they did. All they did.

"Fat chance of that," the slimy man hissed, then commanded, "One step back at a time," as he shoved Mae forward.

"The police are going to be here any second," Jacob's voice came again, sounding calm, and yet, she heard a tone of warning, too. For her sake? Or directed at the man who held her captive?

And where were his father and Susan? Were they still alive?

"No they aren't," Baylor said. "Anyone who tries is going to be stopped by the state police."

Horror-laced fear swept through Mae. They'd known Baylor couldn't be working alone. She'd assumed that he'd had a dirty cop in various local forces. Not that he had some of the state's top cops on his side.

She'd known, even before she could prove that he was part of a large trafficking ring. She hadn't had an idea how huge the scope truly was.

"You willing to take a chance on the fact that my agents, knowing I'm in trouble, are going to bow to the state police?"

"It's either that or get shot," Baylor hissed back, filled with the bravado of a true narcissist. "But you do bring up a good point," the man continued, pushing Mae forward, her only view the wood floor of the upstairs hallway.

"But first, Sam and Susan, thinking they're just going

to flaunt themselves together right in front of me, have to pay for their betrayal," Baylor continued, the evil in his voice sending shivers through Mae's veins. "They'd already be dead if you hadn't interrupted. She's going to watch me kill her lover. And then she goes. I should have done it to her years ago, the traitorous bitch."

Mae could see carpet.

"And then you, my man, are my way out of the state, and then out of the country. You're a fed. And from what I hear, highly trusted. You're going to tell any authority who asks that I came to you when I overheard some guys talking about taking sweet young things out of foster care."

"I am, huh?" Jacob's voice was so deceptively calm then, right at the time the women he and Mae had been angsting over for months had been mentioned.

He was warning her to be ready. To pay attention to him.

To know.

And so, head to the floor, she watched for his feet. And she listened to what he wasn't saying.

Baylor shoved her into the room. "You're going to do whatever it takes to get them to believe that I'm taking you to the boss…"

Mae saw Jacob's foot. Turning slightly to the right. Tapping. Neither of which were normal habits. She tried to concentrate, to hear him, but as Baylor said, "…and helping you rescue all those women…," she just couldn't take anymore.

Turning so harshly she felt hair ripping out of her head, Mae swung up once. Hard. With more force than she'd ever had before, powered by God, by angels, by fate, by feelings for Jacob, she didn't know.

She just knew that she only had one chance to smash the palm of her hand in the exact right spot of Ken Baylor's nose to run his bone up between his eyes.

And so she did.

Jacob heard the gun go off. Thought it was Ken's and that Mae's brave move had been her last. "No!" he hollered so harshly the words scraped his throat.

Susan screamed.

And Jacob dove forward in time to see the blood coming out of the sides of Ken's eyes, and the bullet in the man's side, too. Just as Chay appeared in the room's doorway. A couple of his officers falling in right behind him.

Sirens came from outside. So many Jacob thought he was hearing roaring in his ears. And he saw Mae. Standing, hunched over, with her back to him, staring at the man she'd just taken down with one well-placed blow.

"I learned it in self-defense class," she said, as though lost, and that's when he saw the ugly purpling along her shoulder and the back of her neck.

If Baylor hadn't already been on his back, Jacob would have put him there himself. Reaching Mae, as Chay's men got to Susan, and Sam, Jacob wrapped his arms around her, holding her close, and said softly, "I needed you to step to the right." He was working. They were working. "Just one step and I'd have had a shot of his gun arm. Even if he'd managed to pull the trigger, his shot would have gone in the wall." He'd had a plan.

But she hadn't needed him.

Chapter 22

Mae rode alone in the ambulance. Her doing. While Jacob was with his father, she told her crew they could go. Ken Baylor was still alive, and if he recovered from his wounds, she would need to have every piece of evidence in her lab processed so that he had the rest of his life stolen from him.

And spent it rotting in a cell.

She didn't think she needed the trip to the hospital, but didn't fight the general consensus from Jacob and Chay, and the paramedics, that she should get checked out. There could be a neck or spine injury that was more than just immediate pain, and she'd need to tend to that. No way she was going to risk letting the harm Baylor had done to her have lasting effects. She was not going to carry the man's work on her body around with her for the rest of her life.

And by midafternoon, after hours of sitting up in a hospital bed in an emergency room cubicle, being fussed over, and taken here and there for various tests, she'd been told she was good to go. Just needed to wait for a prescription for pain medications, and for discharge paperwork.

She waited alone. As she'd done for most of the downtime that day. The waiting. She'd always been a bit of a loner. An introvert. Somewhat awkward. Mostly wanted it that way. Until she sat there in the hospital. Knowing that Jacob was with his father. And the rest of the family that she suspected had gathered together in worry for the man who'd fathered them.

The Colton cousins would be there, too. Highlighting for Mae, as she sat alone yearning for her close associate who'd shared the case with her, that he had his family. And she'd shoved hers away.

Slowly throughout that day, as medical personnel had come and gone, with good news each time, Mae's heart had started to crack. And then burst open. Showering her with emotional truths that were as real as any science would ever be. She had family, legal and loving family, who would be there, too, if she'd let someone notify them. All of them. Frazzling her a bit with their need to coddle, and yet…during those hours…a little coddling wouldn't have been all bad.

For a while there, she'd laid her head back against the pillow, and had allowed her absent family to soothe her with memories that bore as much truth as her mass spectrometer. She'd had a solid, secure upbringing, in a nice home filled with kindness, caring, support, opportunity. And unconditional love.

Unlike the fosters. If not for her parents, Mae could have ended up very differently. Their biology might not have created her body, but they'd shaped the person she'd become every step of the way. She hadn't been like them in some ways, and yet they'd helped her to develop into her best self. Giving her the opportunities, the encouragement, the freedom to follow her path.

Still, she hadn't called them. Or asked anyone else to do so. How could she? She'd shunned them. Repeatedly over the past week, but before that, too. Not visiting enough. Making excuses not to accept dinner invitations. Keeping holiday visits as brief as possible. Never inviting them into her world.

Jacob had, though. Because of his call to her mother, William had actually been to the ISB building.

Mae had had one visit, during those hours of waiting that day. Susan Baylor. The woman—who, other than rope burns and some minor bruising, was fine—had stopped in to see her when Sam had been wheeled off for an EKG and some X-rays with only one family member allowed in the room. Susan was the man's girlfriend, not his wife. Sam's eldest child, who had medical power of attorney, had been asked by hospital personnel to accompany him.

Which explained why Mae hadn't seen Jacob all day. Or she pretended it did. But she knew him. The job was done. He was in his personal world and that didn't include her.

Although when Susan, as she'd been leaving, had said, "Jacob has been monitoring every test you had, insisting that he hear the results," Mae had felt an unprofessional jolt that was still with her as she prepared to leave.

She'd been asked, when she'd first been brought in, if there was anyone she wanted to notify, or anyone she wanted to be consulted if she lost consciousness, and she'd named Jacob. Signing a form that allowed him access to her medical information.

Like minds. She'd signed. He'd asked.

He needed her at the lab. And her injury had been work-related. Of course he'd needed to know her progress.

It had still been nice to know that they'd been on the same page. Or at least on ones that were similar enough to get the job done. She'd named him, not with a thought of work, exactly, but just because she'd been in too much pain to discern and he was there, at the hospital.

She got dressed, in jeans and a white, short-sleeved button-down shirt that had come from a cupboard in the emergency room, put there by a charity that kept the cupboard stocked for those who had to have their clothes cut off when they were brought in. Or, like her, had had garments that had just been too soiled to put them back on.

Her own tennis shoes were still wearable.

A testimony to her not-quite-back-yet state of mind came when she was ready to go and realized she didn't have her purse. Or transportation.

She'd arrived at the scene in Jacob's car, not her own. When she'd been told that the vehicles at the house had been transported to the hospital, she'd been thinking she could drive herself home.

Because she hadn't been thinking. While her headache was gone, she wasn't yet back to her normal self. She'd been administered a pain medication she wouldn't be taking again, in spite of the prescription she'd been given. And was obviously a bit less focused than she'd thought.

Planning to call a rideshare to get back to the lab, where she had some cash she could use to pay for it, she was processing the fact that she didn't have her cell phone either, when the door to her small room opened.

Jacob stood there, in very wrinkled uniform pants and shirt, with stubble on his chin, looking so good to her she almost cried.

"Dad's awake," he told her. "He's going to be held overnight for monitoring, due to the concussion, but all of his tests have come back great, so he'll be released tomorrow with no restrictions."

Mae smiled, relieved to hear the news, and because he'd been the one to share it with her, too.

"You ready to go?" he asked then.

Nothing about how she felt, but then from what Susan had said, he'd been getting reports every step of the way. Supposedly to the point of being a bit of a pain to some of the nurses.

About to tell him she was going to call a rideshare, Mae just nodded. He held the door open for her.

Not knowing where he was leading her, and not particularly caring, either, Mae followed him out.

He had her purse in his car. And her phone, too. Chay had dropped the latter off to him when he'd come to give Jacob his incident report—and check on how Mae, Sam, and Susan were doing. Officers had found the phone outside his dad's house, in the shrubbery up by the corner near the front.

Mae hadn't been taken from the car, as he'd thought. She'd been out trying to see if she could help. He didn't ask to verify why she'd been caught where she had. He just knew.

At the moment, he was still too stopped up with fear and anger at what had happened to her to be able to converse with her about all that had occurred.

Turned out, she'd probably been safer her way as she'd given herself the possibility of staying hidden. Had she been sitting in the car, thinking the police were going to be roaring up in seconds, she'd have been easier prey for the ex-politician.

A sitting duck.

Didn't make his lack of preventing Ken Baylor from ever getting his hands on Mae any easier to bear. All day long, he'd avoided looking her in the eye because he hadn't been able to do so openly.

It was time to man up. "I'm sorry, Mae," he told her as he walked her out to his SUV. He'd been told which row it was in. Busied himself with looking for it as they walked. "I never should have left you in the car."

"You did your job, Jacob. And we both believed the police were right behind you." Her tone lacked… Mae. Which made no sense. And yet, the deduction remained.

She was lagging a bit, and he slowed his pace. He'd been told she was fine. That she'd be sore for a few days, but there shouldn't be any lasting repercussions. X-rays of her neck and spine checked out normal. The headache she'd had when they brought her in had been nerve based, due to the blow to her neck. There was no sign of head trauma. Her brain scan had been clean. He'd read every report.

The long day apart from her had been excruciating. He had so much to say. And let her into his vehicle, holding the passenger door for her, closing it, saying none of it.

He'd spent the day where he'd been most needed. But hadn't been where he'd needed to be. It was a situation that had to be dealt with.

Mae had her purse on her lap. Pulling her cell out of

his pocket, he handed it to her. Searched for words. And she said, "Can you take me back to the lab, please? The doctor said I'm okay to drive, and my car's there. Plus, I want to do a little bit in the lab yet. We're going to need as much evidence as I can produce to make certain that there's no loophole through which Baylor can escape."

The job. It was always the job. Except for when it wasn't. Jacob got that loud and clear. He just wasn't sure what to do with it. So, instead of starting the engine, he turned toward her and fell into their comfort zone. "Tomorrow's soon enough to get back to processing everything," he told her. "It's going to be a while before your evidence will be needed in court."

"Baylor's going to live," she said. "I asked."

"The bone didn't pierce his brain," he acknowledged. She'd saved them. Brought down a deranged individual. She hadn't killed a man. He was so damned proud of her he wasn't sure what to do with it all.

Then he added what Ken had already blurted, but he wasn't sure Mae had taken in. "He didn't have a contact in the Dark Canyon department," he started in with the reports he'd been given. "It was the state police, who Dark Canyon, Oso, and other local and county departments across the state trusted and took direction from, who had the mole. Two of them. Both have been arrested."

Mae's mouth tightened. "So, it's over?"

His gaze met hers for the first time since he'd been separated from her that morning, held tight as he gave a slow nod. "You did it, Mae. Not like you'd thought you would, but you ended it."

Her brown eyes moist, but wide open, Mae said, "No, Jacob, *we* did it."

* * *

Mae's newly opened heart was spilling goo all over inside her. She had so much to say. Didn't trust herself to utter a word of it. Not until she had time to compile. To study. To make sense of all the changes going on inside her.

She needed to go home. To sit alone with herself in her space and digest.

Jacob was just sitting there. Not starting the car.

"Your mother called me." His words dropped like little bombs in the car. Splintering the shell that encased her. Encased *them*.

Her fault. She'd taken him to the wedding.

Her whole life was imploding over one split-second opening of her mouth without thought. The day she'd stated Jacob's name as her plus-one for Matilda's wedding.

She hadn't planned to ask him. Had prevaricated for so long. And in a moment of weakness, she'd put things in motion that had escalated beyond control.

She'd had her family's DNA samples for years. Had never done a thing with them. Until being with Jacob at the wedding had left her feeling…lacking.

"The FBI has taken over the case," he told her. "It's been all over the news. Your parents called you, several times." He glanced at the cell phone she'd dropped into her purse. "When they couldn't reach you, they called me."

She hadn't even thought about the news. Or the FBI. "Is the FBI going to take my evidence from me?" She asked the one thing she could process. She had to find the answers for the women whose fate she'd been living with for so many months. To bring them closure.

"No," Jacob told her, his gaze soft as it held hers. "They're going to work with us, and you're still going to be in charge of evidence."

Okay. That felt better. Normal. Good, even. She was going to be working with the FBI. "You said *we*—are you still on it, too?"

"Yes. And Chay will be, too. All of our jurisdictions are heavily involved. The FBI will be solely working on recovery."

Mae heard what he wasn't saying. The missing women would finally be searched for. Mae didn't kid herself that they'd all be found. Most particularly with another country involved. But she knew that some of them would be. And that if even one life was recovered, risking her life had been worth it.

She'd have died just to prevent further lives being stolen.

"Your mom and dad need to see you, Mae. They're pretty distraught."

She nodded. "Take me to my car. I'll call. Maybe have dinner with them." She didn't want to make the drive. Not that night.

But she'd wished they were with her in the hospital.

Jacob didn't start his vehicle. Glancing over at him, she caught him watching her. With a look she couldn't decipher. Frowning, she asked, "What?"

"I already told them I'd bring you to them."

Oh. A little more something good oozed out inside her.

And, nodding, she said, "Okay."

* * *

Jacob didn't plan to stay. As though by mutual agreement, he and Mae discussed the case the entire way to her folks' farm. He'd prepared himself to watch her get out of the SUV and walk away from him. To walk into her family's embrace while he headed back to the office to get started on all the paperwork the day had generated.

Instead, she'd remained seated next to him, insisting that he come with her, and as her mom, dad, and brothers came hurrying out to his vehicle, surrounding them on both sides, he'd done so.

The plan had been for her to stay with her parents for a day or two. At least.

Mae hadn't agreed to that, either. Saying she hadn't been to her apartment in over a week and needed to water her plants.

The comment was somewhat absurd, given the circumstances, but all Mae. And after a home-cooked meal, lots of spilling of the beans where Mae was concerned, and more laughter than he'd ever have expected, she was once again sitting next to Jacob for the drive back to Dark Canyon.

He wasn't prepared. Hadn't found any words to get things back to normal between them. And spent the entire trip back driving the SUV, and the conversation. Keeping her talking about the various things her family had brought up. And the memories she shared that grew from them.

He drove to the ISB building because it made sense. It was the space they shared, the only place where they belonged together. And where her car was parked.

Pulling up to her vehicle, positioning the SUV so that

her driver's door was right next to his passenger door, he put his vehicle in Park, but didn't shut it off.

She glanced at him. He looked back. Filled with conflicting thoughts. Feelings he couldn't pin down. Or even understand. And then she nodded, reached for the door handle, slid off the seat to the ground, put her purse on her shoulder, and said, "See you in the morning," before shutting the door.

Sitting there, Jacob watched her open her own car door, get in, put on her seat belt. And, seconds later, drive away.

There'd be more work. The recovery effort with the FBI. Other ISB cases.

But they'd nailed Baylor.

The case was done.

The first thing Mae did after she dropped her purse on the table where it lived inside her apartment was water her plants.

The can was right where she'd left it. She filled it as she always did. And in the same order as always, made her way around the five rooms, silently checking over each of the living items in her home, giving them sustenance.

Refusing to cry.

She'd nearly completed the task when her doorbell rang, sending a shock of terror to her heart. She never had visitors.

And what if they'd all been wrong and there was another player out there? One who wanted to stop her from finding critical proof?

Gun in hand, cocked and ready, she stayed out of window range and, back to walls, made her way to the door. With one eye squeezed tightly shut, she peered through the peephole.

And nearly dropped the gun in relief.

With it hanging from her right hand, she unlocked and pulled open the door with her left.

"What did I forget?" she asked Jacob. He'd never visited her at home in the past, but he'd been there to get clothes just that week. And with the hell they'd been through over the past couple of days, it just didn't feel odd that he'd stop by to take care of business rather than wait until morning.

He had a lot of wrapping up to do.

"You forgot to kiss me goodbye."

She stared. Certain she'd misheard him. That her brain was more rattled than she'd realized. She was hearing things. Or making them up.

Because she had no idea what he was actually talking about, she stood there. Mute. Looking him in the eyes to try to figure out what was going on.

Jacob's eyes had been talking to her since the first day she'd met him. He hadn't wanted such a young forensic scientist in his lab. He'd wanted someone with more experience.

Then.

At the moment, he wanted something very different. He stepped up to her, guiding her gently backward with his hands on her hips, his body pressing against hers, and then lowered his head.

His lips didn't just cover Mae's, they consumed them.

Hers did his, too.

They'd always been honest with each other. Some communications didn't include words.

She heard her front door close. Felt his arms wrap all the way around her waist, as her hands lifted up to lock tightly around his neck.

They might make it to the bedroom. Or do it right there on the floor. They had to end the case.

All parts of it.

Had to get it out of their systems.

So it made no sense that he suddenly pulled away.

Until it did.

They'd solved the case, but the sex experiment had failed. He was there to deal with that. As the boss, he had to have figured out that they couldn't go forth into a new day, a new case, without resolving the physical situation between them.

Except that, the scientist in her—the woman in her—suddenly knew that, for her, there was no way that was ever going to happen.

Jacob was still there. Still holding her. Just not body to body. He was looking into her eyes. And when she reluctantly looked back, opening herself up fully to the honesty between them, to his unspoken words, she frowned.

Was seeing messages she'd never seen before. Was almost afraid to try to decipher them for fear of being wrong.

And almost as though sensing that, he said, "I've never once been in a serious relationship."

"I know." She hadn't, either. But the moment wasn't about her.

"It just never felt right."

Again, she agreed. Nodded. Was glad that they were

going to be able to end things while still loosely attached, and in agreement.

Even while her heart was hurting worse than it had at any other time in her life. Way more than when she'd seen her biological test results.

"Somewhere over the past couple of years, I ceased even considering myself as marriage material because at thirty-three, I've never met a woman who I felt the least bit toward as my parents had clearly felt toward each other, even in the end when Mom was so sick. Especially then."

She got it. Didn't need to hear anymore. But he was her… Jacob. And if he needed to talk, she'd listen. No matter how hard doing so turned out to be.

"But it wasn't just love," he said slowly, and Mae frowned. Confused again.

"They were best friends," Jacob said. "Like… Nick and Sassy."

He stopped then. Staring intently into her eyes.

Sassy. His cousin. Who'd done her hair. And brought them food. Who'd recently realized that she was in love with her best friend.

And… "Jacob?" Mae asked. Her eyes filling with tears. They came from nowhere. And seemed to be everywhere. Inside her as much as out.

"I don't want the case to end, Mae," he said. "I want the evil to end, Baylor's reign to end. But the case… this…us… I can't imagine a way where going back, losing this, not being a part of your personal life, going to weddings with you, eating with you regularly…will work."

Right then, in that second, Mae's internal spectrometer spoke loud and clear. Giving her the results she'd been avoiding, hiding from, for far too long. "I love you, Jacob Colton," she said, and then, she just continued giving it up. "I think I fell in love on the first case we ever worked, when I'd only given you half the results and you understood..."

He kissed her before she could finish, and Mae told him what she'd been going to say, and so much more, as she mingled her mouth with his, her tongue with his, and a short time later, her body with his, too.

There would bumps along their way. Situations and issues that they'd have to figure out. Some words to speak, too.

And answers to find.

But they'd found their bottom line.

They were two people who dealt in fact every day of their lives.

And the fact was, they belonged together.

Epilogue

His dad was getting married, and Jacob was right beside him. The best man. Six months ago, he'd never have seen himself standing at the head of the church, in full tuxedo gear, smiling as his father and Susan promised to love each other until death did them part.

It went beyond the physical designation, though. He knew.

Love didn't end. His father's love for his mother. And Susan's love for Kate Colton, too. Love was able to see beyond the human beings it gifted, to speak through them, and to hold them even when they didn't know they were being held.

Susan had chosen Dr. Mae Copeland to stand with her, for the ceremony. Mae had done what Susan had been unable to do. She'd brought Ken Baylor, who'd abused the woman for years, to his knees. But in her own way, Susan had, too. She'd hidden a key years before, held on to it, even if she hadn't known why, and remembered it in time.

As his dad and new stepmom said their own personal vows, Jacob glanced just beyond them, and saw Mae looking straight at him. She was stunningly gorgeous in the long gray sheath that hugged her slender curves to perfection. And the hair…loose, long, the curls flowing like angels around her…the makeup that Sassy had done full out… Mae could have been on any modeling stage. Or graced the pages of any glamour magazine.

Jacob smiled at her. His eyes telling her that he preferred the sexy scientist who'd had her way with him in her lab.

He wasn't certain, but he was pretty sure she was mentally sticking her tongue out at him. With a promise for as many repeats as his manly form could endure.

He was up for every one of them. Which he leaned over and whispered to her as they walked, arm in arm, back down the aisle behind the newlyweds and out to a fairy-tale-looking reception in the softly lighted twilight grounds beyond. Tables were set with linens in the manicured area of grass and garden behind the church. A buffet was being catered by Susan's own business. A small dance floor had been laid, with a microphone set up to the sound system that played soft music in the background.

Holding Mae's hand, Jacob made a beeline for Chay, his good friend, and a man he rarely felt the need to mess with as he did with his little brothers.

Chay's new wife, Ava, Jacob's cousin, was busy talking to Fern, who'd been glowing since Baylor's arrest, and who'd been seen with another of Jacob's cousins—Ryan, the firefighter who'd rescued her and saved her life—pretty much everywhere she went.

While baby Ella Grace jabbered happy gibberish on Ava's lap, Chay, standing just behind his wife's chair, said, "Fern was just saying that she's training as a 911 dispatcher."

And before Jacob could respond, Mae piped in—so unlike her—with, "I'm glad. It means she'll be working closely with Ryan." After which she took her and Jacob's joined hands behind his back, and while still holding his fingers, softly pinched his butt.

Because…turned out…working with someone who was your world—luckily for them there were no rules against doing so—was the best life ever.

Unaware of what was going on behind his back, Chay elbowed Jacob at the same. "What's with your other cousin over there?" he asked, pointing at Sassy, who was currently locked in a clearly passionate kiss. "I'm glad she and Nick finally admitted they loved each other, but, get a room, you know?"

Jacob rolled his eyes.

And Ava turned around to say, "I think it's sweet. This entire town's been watching them pal around for most of their lives. It's nice of them to share the happy ending with us."

"As long as they keep it PG rated," Noah said, as he and Sabrina, glasses of champagne in hand, joined them. Jacob's baby brother and his US Forest Service officer girlfriend were actually out without their K-9s for once. Jacob kind of missed the presence of the service dogs.

And made a note to talk to Mae about getting a pet.

One who'd be happy living in her lab a good bit of the time.

"By the way," Noah said then, looking around the group, as Ryan sat down next to Fern, rubbing her back. "Sabrina and I are getting married a little sooner than planned."

The way his brother looked at his intended bride warned Jacob that more was coming. Just as Sabrina said, "I'm pregnant!" With a huge grin on her face.

Jacob felt Mae stumble for a second next to him. And

he knew that there would be an upcoming conversation soon about the topic of parenthood. Probably in the lab.

One that he'd have expected himself to dread, to avoid however possible, even a month before.

But as he stood there with his family, watching his father and Susan move around among their close friends, Jacob found himself almost ready for the conversation.

Almost.

Dinner was announced and he and Mae joined the queue going through the buffet line. And took part in the conversations going on at their table, too. A lot of the time, along with Chay, answering questions about some of the women they'd found, with the FBI's help. A couple of who had been in transport and hadn't yet been sold.

As he sat there, eating delicious food, Jacob was happier than he'd ever been. More content then he'd ever been.

More alive.

And yet, he couldn't help noticing the empty chairs at the next table. His brother Mark, the bodyguard, and Mark's nurse girlfriend, Cassidy, were late. Which was very unlike them. They'd been visiting their distant Colton relatives in North Dakota, but had assured Sam that they'd be back in time for the wedding.

Even as Jacob felt a stab of concern, the couple came around the side of the church, hand in hand. Jacob watched as they went straight for Sam and Susan, watched the smiles on their faces as they congratulated the couple, and then got in line for food.

His family was together. All was good.

And yet, he wasn't surprised when Mark, plate in hand, took the long way to his chair, to stop behind Jacob, lean down, and say, "There's some trouble in North Dakota," before continuing on to his seat.

Jacob had known there had to have been a good reason for Mark's tardiness.

"You can follow up tomorrow," Mae leaned over to tell him, the serious look in her gaze telling him that she'd do what she could as well.

He kissed her then and there. Long and full. Appropriate or not. He loved the woman. It was what it was.

And then one of Sam's friends was at the microphone saying that it was time to throw the bouquet.

And Jacob was ready to go. To get Mae to himself. At his condo. Her apartment. Her lab, he wasn't particular. He just needed some experiment time with the woman who made him more than he'd ever been.

Leaning over, he whispered, "You ready to get naked?"

The look of steamy desire that she sent him was her answer. They stood, with everyone else, and had taken a couple of steps toward the SUV when something flew right at them. Before Jacob could intercept it, the flying object landed in Mae's hands.

The bouquet.

His family, their friends let out whistles and cheers. Catcalls, too.

And with a grin at all of them, Jacob put his arm around Mae, felt her arm slide around him, and, bouquet in her hand, they left.

To live the life they'd been born to.

Together.

* * * * *